Family Trees

by

Aurelio O'Brien

Bad Attitude Books, Altadena, California

ISBN: 978-1-935927-31-0

In loving memory of my big sister, Mary,

who always saw the good in me.

Holidays are exclamation points in life's long narrative. Whether they punctuate happy or sad years, hectic or tranquil events, they don't stand in isolation from all the baggage the rest of the year has dragged into them.

What costume to wear for Halloween is a reaction to each year's cultural trends and can be fraught with weighty contemplation or become an opportunity to personify timely fears or topical humor.

Who gets invited to Thanksgiving dinner, where to seat them and next to whom—all depend on that year's family dynamics.

What to get for Christmas gifts and how much to spend on each recipient (and who actually makes your list) are a response to each year's personal budget and the recipient's behavior toward you throughout that year. If the person was especially kind, you may want to do something extra-nice, if they have been an irritation, then their gift might be seen as an opportunity to make that clear.

Holidays may be celebrated nationally or internationally, but they are, within one's own family circle, taken *personally*. And, like tree rings, each yearly celebration adds a new layer to every family's growth.

This story explores how an untimely tragedy punctuated one family's holiday seasons.

Chapter One

Deforestation

The street lights were aglow that misty Monday morning. It was during the quiet aftermath of the long holiday season, when the New Year had already passed by on the calendar but hadn't yet begun to actually sink in.

Oak Drive, a comfortable suburban street of superficially varied middle-class post-WWII tract homes stuffed mostly with two-parent baby-boomed families mid-way through living out their American dreams, was still hung-over from the serial celebrations. These homes lay dark and silent, revealing no eagerness from any of their occupants to resume normal work or school schedules or to face their obligatory fresh lists of New Year's resolutions.

The large, two-story Benjamin house was located appropriately mid-block, for theirs was that designated home every decent mid-1960's suburban street required—a social hub where neighborhood kids gathered for afternoon treats, street ball games, general mayhem, and late evening hide-and-go-seek.

This was all true because Ellen Benjamin lived there. Back-handedly complimented by the other mothers on Oak Drive as "that woman with the six only-children," they didn't mind if their kids joined her six while she spoiled them all rotten with home-baked afterschool snacks and glasses of milk, repaired any skinned knees, or helped them with their school projects as long as she kept them out of their hair. In addition to a well-stocked first-aid kit, the Benjamins kept ample supplies of toys, board games, and crafting materials. With the Benjamin kid's ages evenly spaced—ranging from four to fifteen—no neighborhood kid of any age ever felt the

1

least bit out of place hanging out at their house.

Ellen grew up on a farm; she took on both her wifely duties and motherhood with well-trained nurturing proficiency. On the farm she worked with her folks to raise better grain, vegetables, and livestock. Her job as an adult was to rear a new generation of better people. Rather than emphasizing "The Three R's"—that was for schoolteachers—Ellen dubbed her own self-invented educational theory "The Three C's: Curiosity, Creativity, and Craft."

She also cooked and cleaned and sewed and ironed and packed six nutritious lunches each school day with the skill and dedication of a fine artist.

Her husband, Ed, was her enabler, willing to let her live out her child-rearing dreams. Having so many kids was not really his thing, too chaotic, unruly, and disorderly for his mind that preferred the tidy numbers and formulas of aerospace engineering. But Ellen enabled his goals right back and was just as devoted to spoiling him as rotten as she did all their kids, so why complain? It also helped that he had fallen head-over-heels in love with her. She was quite impossible for anyone to resist. She was innately attractive, clever, funny, resourceful, loving, and passionate. Until only recently, theirs had been the perfect marriage, the perfect family, the perfect American dream.

Ed's domestic job list was short and simple in comparison to hers: provide a decent income and keep the lawns and gardens green and tidy. The front planter was lined with Christmas poinsettias he had planted right after Thanksgiving—a holiday tradition he and Ellen began when they first bought the house. A station wagon that could comfortably carry all eight of them sat in the driveway. The bills were all paid off, except the mortgage. So far, so good.

In truth, the lawns needed mowing and Ed still hadn't taken the Christmas lights down from the eaves. It was on his New Year's to-do list. He'd get to it. At least the Christmas tree was down and put to the curb. Since Ellen had been diagnosed with breast cancer and had her double-mastectomy, his routine was knocked off kilter and his priorities had shifted.

Only the two eldest kids, Ann and Frank, were aware of just how seriously ill their mother was—Ellen and Ed felt it served no purpose to burden the younger ones with it. Ellen was good at pretending everything was fine. And she honestly believed she would recover. She was still young. She prayed and hoped the surgery got all of the cancer out; she held faith that everything would go back to normal very soon. The holidays this year had worn her down more than usual, but she'd feel better again now that it was all over.

Lining the sidewalks of Oak Drive, each household had obediently placed their trash cans to the curb along with their discarded Christmas trees, for this was the officially-designated tree disposal day—when the waste service brought an extra truck.

The front door of the still-dark Benjamin house cracked open and the six Benjamin kids slipped stealthily out into the brisk morning air, accompanied by their shaggy mongrel, Chaos, and their once-stray tabby, Mommacat.

Just then, the street lights clicked off, as if to signal, "Go."

The eldest boy, Frank, checked his watch.

"Hurry!" he whispered.

It was tacitly understood that they were on a tight schedule. They didn't want any of the other kids on the block stealing their great idea or beating them to it.

Three of them dashed up the block as two others and Chaos dashed down it while Matty Benjamin, the youngest, stood in the middle of their front lawn watching his breath make clouds while batting his arms against his sides in an effort to stay warm, with Mommacat stropping at his leg.

Matty wandered to the front edge of the lawn to glance up the street. His jaw went slack as he beheld two dry Christmas trees quickly waddling up the sidewalk toward him shedding a trail of dry needles. He glanced down the street to see three more trees headed his way. As they reached the lawn the trick was revealed to him that they were all being carried by his older siblings, and he clapped in appreciation.

"Shh!" Frank scolded.

Ann, the eldest Benjamin and only girl, whispered directions to each of her brothers, artfully arranging the trees here and there across their lawn. Frank darted into the garage to get some bits of lumber, tent stakes, and heavy twine to prop up any trees in need of support. Trip after trip they made, with the efficiency and relentlessness of army ants, until their front lawn had become a kind of mildly sad, yet undeniably impressive, post-Christmas tree forest.

Then came the distant sound of a trash truck opening its bin.

"Just in time," Frank noted.

"We did it," Ann sighed, smiling.

The Benjamin kids gaped in awe at the dense forest they had created together. No one else on their block had one—probably no one else anywhere in the world.

Sure, some of the trees had needleless limbs, broken ornaments, and bits of crinkled lead tinsel hanging here and there; the few with flocking were shedding their fake snow. All in all, they were a mismatched ensemble: some were tall, others short, some fat and full, others lean and spindly, two were completely toast-brown and one from Miss Toulie's trash, flocked with cotton-candy pink fluff. Ann placed it just left of center to function as a focal point.

Chaos lifted his leg on the pink one—everyone's a

critic.

But still, it was a marvel to behold.

As they wandered through it, the last wisps of morning mist burned away and the sun peeked over the distant hills to slowly illuminate the tips of their trees. It soon set the tinsel-bits sparkling and cut long shadows across the lawn, giving the whole tableau added dimensional depth, and the kids gasped in renewed awe at their creation.

Mommacat suddenly and inexplicably jerked and ran away, startling Matty.

The deep grinding and clunking sounds of the approaching trash truck was soon cut by the piercing wail of a siren. As the siren grew nearer, the kids heard their father's muffled voice inside the house bark out their names in order of age:

"Ann! Frank! Randy! Tony! Benny! Matty!"

"What did we do wrong *now?*" Tony sighed.

The siren grew louder and nearer. The smaller kids put their fingers in their ears. An ambulance rounded the corner and pulled to a stop directly in front of their house.

The kids stood frozen as the front door burst open and Ed Benjamin called out, "In here!" motioning for the white coated attendants to bring their gurney up the front walk and into the house.

Frank and Ann shared looks of surprised concern.

Roused by the sirens, lights flicked on in neighborhood houses and several curious neighbors peeked through windows or from doorways to discover what the commotion was about.

Moments later the whitecoats wheeled their mother out, followed by their father carrying her small suitcase. He was about to toss it into the car, but stopped short, finally taking in the forest.

"What the hell is all *this*?!" he barked.

"We... made a forest," Ann explained.

"Get rid of it! **Now!**"

"But, they were free," Randy, the second-eldest boy, chimed in, providing a rationale.

"We didn't make it for you," Benny, the second-youngest sassed back. "We made it for *Mom*."

"Ed, please," they heard their mother sigh, causing their dad to droop his shoulders, shake his head, and retreat.

Ellen asked the attendants to wait a minute. She lifted herself to her elbows and turned her to her kids, smiling.

"It's beautiful. I *love* it."

Ellen motioned for Ann to come to her.

She sank back onto the gurney and took Ann's hand in both of hers.

Her mother's hands felt cold and her skin was pale. Anne could feel herself starting to cry, but for her mom's sake she fought the tears back.

Ellen squeezed her daughter's hand and looked her straight in the eye.

"Take care of your dad and brothers," she whispered.

"I will."

"I love you, Annie."

Ellen let go and the attendants loaded her into the rear of the ambulance.

Ed motioned Frank over. He gave him a stern look and pointed to the trees.

"Those! Gone by the time I get back!"

"Yessir."

The ambulance pulled away with its siren wailing again, followed by Ed in the station wagon.

6

"They never called an ambulance before," Frank whispered to Ann.

"It'll be okay," Ann assured, as much for herself as for him.

The trash truck reached their house and the garbage men quickly emptied their cans into the truck's hopper before the regular truck moved on. The extra tree truck followed it, but not seeing their tree at their curb with their cans, started to move on too.

"Wait! *Wait!* Wait!" the kids all screamed, each frantically dragging a tree to the curb.

A crisp, dry October dawn arrived on Oak Drive.

Less than two years had passed since the kids created and dismantled their magical forest all in one morning. The magic hadn't worked—their mother never came back from the hospital. The following Christmas then became the Christmas that wasn't; it seemed as if Christmas itself had died right along with her.

The Benjamin house looked forlorn and tired this year. The half-dead strings of Christmas lights had stayed up year-round since Ellen's death and the poinsettias had long ago shriveled to husks save one stubborn plant that wasn't having any of it and was now the size of a small tree. The kids knew better than to mention any of these things to their dad. They also didn't mention the now weedy yard and patchy lawn, whenever they actually bothered to notice these things; these weren't seen as problems to them because, as Benny pointed out, their dad would just have to put the lights back up again each Christmas anyway, and the gangly poinsettia had earned its right to remain, and the weeds were far more interesting plants than boring old

7

grass.

Neighborhood kids no longer gathered at the Benjamin house to play or socialize. Without Ellen to dole out treats and attention, and with the other parents now labeling the Benjamin household as "unsupervised," their house was basically taboo. The Benjamins weren't really all too bothered by that either; there were more than enough of them to organize, build, or play anything they wanted to all on their own.

Ed's alarm clock rang and his big feet hit the floor almost simultaneously—it was both his army training and engineer's brain that made him find some solace in routine: each and every school day he'd stomp down the ice-cold upstairs hallway while still tying on his robe to turn up the thermostat and pound a fist twice on each door he passed to bark, "Frank! Randy! Reveille!" and "Tony! Benny! Matty! Up and at'em!" He'd always rap with his knuckles on Ann's door at the far end of the hallway, rather than pound, following with, "Annie! Time to get up!"

Ed was frugal—with six growing kids he *had* to be. Why heat the house at night when everyone is under blankets in bed? It wasted energy. So, he turned the central heating completely off at bedtime and then turned it back on at daybreak.

Frank questioned this practice and was pretty sure it actually took even more energy to defrost the house every morning than it would if his dad simply maintained reasonable warmth throughout the night, but he hadn't yet bothered to crunch the numbers in order to make a formal argument to him about it.

Ed's routine continued in the kitchen, where he scooped ground coffee from a tin into the aluminum

8

strainer of his electric percolator and started it brewing before stomping back upstairs to shave, shower, and dress for the office, rapping and pounding a second time on Ann's and the boys' doors as he passed them with, "C'mon, Ann! Let's go, boys!"

Eight-year-old Benny climbed down from his top bunk while six-year-old Matty was still drooling on his pillow beneath him. Across the room, twelve-year-old Tony rolled over with a muffled grunt.

Benny crossed to his dresser drawer, but finding it virtually empty, save one lone sock missing its mate, he roamed the moguls of clothes flowing out from their closet floor in search of anything still clean enough to wear again.

Finding nothing suitable, he scampered downstairs, balancing on his heels across the bitingly-frozen kitchen linoleum, to enter the laundry room, which also doubled as his oldest brother Frank's workshop.

Frank, still in his pajamas and bathrobe, was just leaving, carrying a 6 volt battery, an old Model T coil, and some wires.

Frank ignored Benny and Benny knew better than to ask.

Benny opened the dryer, excavated a clean pair of matching socks, briefs, and a badly crumpled pair of jeans from the neglected load within. He removed his pajamas, tossed them in the hamper, and slipped into the briefs, socks, and jeans. He dug around in the dryer again for a suitable shirt. Finding none, he pulled over a step-stool and opened the washing machine to peer in.

"Great."

He held up the damp striped tee shirt he was seeking and snorted. He climbed down and quickly piled the load of dry clothes on top of the dryer to then fill it with the damp load from the washer, and clicked it on.

Shirtless and freezing, he dashed from the laundry room to the hallway closet and extracted his quilted jacket. He zipped it on over his bare torso. It was so cold in the house he could see his breath.

"Jeezus, Dad."

He scampered to the living room and looked behind the couch where the floor heating vent sat, startling Tony, who was already dressed for the day and comfortably seated atop it.

"This one's taken."

Benny dashed off in search of a vacant vent.

Regaining his privacy, Tony slid a *Playboy* magazine out from under the couch to peruse it with lascivious gasps and sighs.

Still snug in her room, Ann sat in her bed writing an entry in her diary. Her hair was in curlers and wrapped in a plastic cap. Her electric hair dryer was on too, but the hot air tube was detached from the cap and blowing under her covers to warm her feet instead.

Thursday, October, 27, 1966

Eight more months until graduation. I can't wait to get out of this madhouse and into college.

Ann stopped writing and slipped a photograph out of the front flap of her diary: a slightly out of focus and badly framed one of her with her mother. Ann was about ten years old. Her mom was hugging her close and they were laughing at something—Ann couldn't remember what; most likely at the irony of her engineer Dad's inability to ever figure out the settings on his camera.

She went back to her entry to add:

I miss Momma.

She slipped the picture back under the flap and latched her diary, tucking it deep in between her mattress and box spring for safe keeping and away from the prying eyes of her nosy brothers.

Figuring all of them should be done using the bathroom by now, she clicked off the hair dryer, slipped into her chenille robe and fuzzy slippers and reached for her door knob.

"*Yeow!*"

The knob delivered a crisp snap of electricity causing her to shriek and jerk back in pain.

She removed her plastic head cap and wrapped it around her hand to open the knob safely. She stomped into the hallway.

Frank and Randy were at the far end of the hall, rolling on the floor in hysterics.

"Frank!" she growled.

Ann looked at the wires, coil, and battery clipped to the outside of her doorknob. She yanked the wires loose, turned, and gave both Frank and Randy the slow burn while heading to the bathroom door with a terse, "I'm telling Dad."

She reached for the bathroom knob, stopped herself, and once again wrapped her hand in her plastic hair cap before turning the knob, sending her brothers into renewed hysterics.

"*I'm telling Dad,*" Randy mimicked, punctuating it with a snort.

Ed stood at the kitchen counter simultaneously eating a bowl of Wheaties, drinking his second cup of coffee, scanning his morning newspaper, and preparing a tuna-noodle casserole.

Randy, Tony, Benny, and Matty were all seated at the kitchen table—a table their father had fashioned out of a hardware store door blank and pre-fab legs—he hadn't been able to find a table large enough, or cheap enough, so necessity became the mother of repurposing.

Randy finished his cereal and pondered aloud, "I need to get rich."

"Don't we all," Ed mumbled back.

"I'm serious, Dad."

Randy lofted his bowl to drink the chocolate milk left over from his Cocoa Krispies. He poured a small amount of Cheerios into his empty bowl and crossed to the refrigerator to add a limp carrot and some lettuce to it, then put the bowl in a bird cage on the sideboard containing not birds, but two rats he had adopted from the science lab at the end of the previous school year: Mucklethorpe and Chocolate Drop.

"Good looking women only like men with lots of money," Tony offered.

Ed glanced sideways at him. "Z'that so?"

"I read it... *somewhere*," Tony explained.

"Everyone knows *that*, Dad," Randy agreed. "That's why I've decided to make movies," he continued. "Then I'll get rich *and* women will flock to me."

Matty laughed, snorting milk out of his nose.

"*Euww!* Matty!" Benny yelped, jumping back.

Ed grabbed a wad of paper towel and wiped up both Matty and the table. He returned to wrap his casserole in Saran and stow it in the fridge.

Ann entered, her hair ratted up, rounded off, and sprayed stiff into a tidy Patty Duke. She scanned the room for Frank, saw Randy—*scowled at him*—grabbed the bottle of milk off the table, then reaching across her father to nab the box of Carnation Instant Breakfast and a clean glass from the upper cupboards.

"Daddy...?" she inquired.

Ed sidled around her to tape a note on the oven door, reading, "5:00 at 350°," then thumbtacked another, larger note with all their names on it but Matty's to the cork board on the wall next to the kitchen table.

"These are your chores for after school—I want them all **done** before I get home."

Ed turned to Ann.

"Get Matty's coat."

Ann glanced at her siblings. With the house *still* not yet comfortably warm *everyone* already wore their coats, as usual.

She rolled her eyes and answered, "He's wearing it," leaving off the implied, "Duh."

Ed opened the fridge again to grab his and Matty's labeled lunch bags from the pile.

He glanced at his watch.

"Matty, let's move."

"Dad," Ann tried again, as she pulled a bag of dog food from under the sink to dump some in a dog bowl next to the sliding glass doors where an eager Chaos pawed the slobber-smeared glass until Ann let him in to scarf down his food.

A couple of kittens darted in with him before she could slide the door closed again.

"Will you *please* listen? Frank wired a battery to my doorknob."

This time Randy laughed, shooting orange juice out of his nose, which was followed up by an, "*Ow!*" from acid-burn. His brothers laughed at him.

"Serves you right," Ann snapped at Randy. She turned back to her dad and continued, "Frank tried to electrocute me and... and... you don't even *care!*"

13

"You can't electrocute someone with a battery. Come on, Matty, we need to go."

Ann shot her dad a pout. He deadpanned back for a moment, then hollered, "FRANK...?!"

No response.

Ed shrugged dismissively at his daughter.

Matty got up and opened the sliding glass doors again, letting in several more kittens.

"This house is a *mess*," Ed groused.

Matty reentered the house carrying a potted marigold followed by a round-bellied Mommacat.

"Mommacat's preggo **again?**" Tony interjected.

"Matty, NOW! Let's go!"

"But I have to feed Lugee."

Matty opened the two lowest kitchen drawers to use as a step stool in order to reach a decimated potted plant on the window sill above the sink. He extracted a large banana slug from the eaten plant and placed it in the fresh one.

"I wish you'd help out more around here," Ed complained to Ann.

"I've got school too! I can't do everything! We need a housekeeper!"

"No housekeeper! If you kids would all just do what I ask...."

She huffed, grabbed the dead plant from Matty's hands, shoved Matty at him, crossed to the sliding glass door, opened it again, tossed the dead plant, pot and all, behind a hedge, closed the door, dusted her hands, and replied, "There. See? I'm helping. Now what about Frank?!"

"**FRANK...?!**" Ed hollered again.

At the house next door, Mrs. Coe swept stray leaves and debris off the far end of her porch, brushing them into the Benjamin's untidy front yard where they'd not be noticed while she eavesdropped. She was never a fan of the Benjamins even when Ellen was alive, considering her "litter" of children to be "so plebeian." She never let her only son, Ross, play with any of the Benjamin kids—or any other kids on the block, for that matter.

Ross was a freakishly large boy for his age and was the block bully, as weird and mean as his mother, so other kids didn't want to play with him anyway. They called him "Ross-Coe, Bosco" or just plain "Bosco" behind his back.

Mrs. Coe stopped sweeping to listen in on Ed's muffled calls for Frank, shaking her head and *tsk*ing in disapproval.

"FRANK! Where the hell are you?! ***FRANK...?!***"

Chapter Two

Outside the Box

Frank tucked his bike between a ficus hedge and the cinderblock wall enclosing the far end of Jefferson High School's parking lot in order to hide it. He then sidled the rest of the way along the wall to peek out from behind the hedge at the lot's entrance.

He was early enough—the parking lot was still deserted.

He dashed across it and into a shadowy covered walkway, zig-zagging from bush to bush toward the school's main building, while the theme music from the TV show, *Mission Impossible*, ran through his head.

Frank ducked behind a mock orange and froze when heard an approaching *scree-scree-scree* sound emanating from inside the main building.

A door latch clicked.

The night janitor, Mr. Harley, clunked his squeaky cleaning cart out the double metal doors ahead of him. He turned, pulled forward his retractable key ring, locked the doors tight, and *scree-scree-scree*-ed off down the exterior hallway.

Frank waited until the squeaking and Mr. Harley turned a corner before dashing to the double doors. Using his scout knife's largest blade, he popped the latch on the door and slipped inside.

He entered a darkened classroom and crossed to the chalkboard. Using the edge of the felt eraser, he scraped it along the chalkboard's rail, carefully collecting a substantial pile of chalk dust into a folded piece of paper at the end of the rail, smiling.

The Jefferson High parking lot was full and the halls were teeming with students by the time Frank remounted his hidden bike and blended himself in among his fellow cycling schoolmates as if he had only just arrived at school along with them. He parked and locked his bike as normal, and entered the main building feigning the same blank look of disinterest most of the kids wore before first period.

When he reached his locker, his sister Ann was there waiting for him.

"I told Dad."

"And... I'm in big trouble, right?"

Ann folder her arms and slumped against the row of lockers.

"No."

"It was a joke," Frank laughed. "Lighten up, sis. You know what they tell us: high school is the happiest time of your life!"

Ann squinched her face in disgust, began to leave, but turned back.

"Your jokes are mean and you're mean."

She spun to leave and banged into Mr. Pratt, a pear-shaped teacher with an exceptionally large rear, rolling his way down the crowded hallway.

"Watch out," Mr. Pratt scolded.

"Sorry," Ann mumbled, adding, "Jerk," under her breath.

"Good morning, Mr. Pratt," Frank replied and waved after him with exaggerated cheeriness.

Mr. Pratt spit out a, "Mornin', Frank," without turning while he continued his voyage down the hallway, dislodging more students in his wake.

Frank grinned to himself. Ann caught the grin.

"You *did* something to him."

"Why would you think that?" Frank smirked back.

"You know, you'd be a lot happier if you'd just try to do something nice for people every once in a while."

Frank batted his eyes at her in innocently.

"Okay, from now on I'll be just like you, Pollyanna."

"Right."

Ed pulled his car into the driveway of The Saint Helena's Convent behind several other cars dropping off children for day care. Sister Louise, a short, round, rosy-cheeked nun, was on duty greeting the arriving children.

"Grab your lunch, and behave yourself today, Matty." Ed ordered.

"I will."

He pulled to a stop in front of Sister Louise. Matty climbed out of the car. Sister Louise greeted Matty and took his hand, but before Ed could pull away, she waved for him to remain.

Sister Louise walked around to his window. Ed cranked it down.

"Good morning, Sister Louise. Is there a problem?"

"Sister Paula requires a brief word with you," she answered, glancing down at Matty and then back at Ed.

Ed checked his watch and furrowed his brow.

"Can't it wait, Sister? I'm running late as it is."

"I don't think so."

Ed set his brake and turned off the car.

"Okay."

He got out and made a quick pace for Sister Paula's office.

Matty broke free from Sister Louise's hand to chase his father down.

"Dad! Dad! *Dad!*"

"What is it, Matty?" Ed stopped, checked his watch again, then looked down.

Matty looked up at him, doe-eyed. With his light brown curls and round blue eyes he looked like one of the chapel's painted cherubs—and he knew it.

"Could I please have a penny?"

"Will you promise to be a good boy today?"

Matty nodded back.

Ed handed him a penny as Sister Louise caught up, taking Matty's hand again.

"Sister is waiting," she reminded Ed.

Ed sorted through crayon sketches depicting piles of bloody severed heads and limbs, impaled bodies, and corpses with X's for eyes that Sister Paula had laid out for him on her desk. He looked questioningly at Sister Paula who pursed her lips.

"They're Matty's recent drawings. He does them quite regularly. We're all very concerned. Especially Sister Louise. She's studied psychology."

Sister Paula collected up the disturbing drawings and put them back in their manila folder. She walked to the other side of her desk to sit. Ed sat down to face her.

"Mutilations, blood, torture." She placed a hand to her forehead and lidded her eyes, saying a silent prayer for Matty's soul.

Past Sister Paula, Ed caught sight of a particularly gruesome painting of a multiply-impaled and bleeding Saint Sebastian hanging on the wall directly behind her.

Sister Paula stopped praying and asked, "Where can he be getting such horrible ideas?"

Ed shifted his eyes from the painting to Sister Paula's earnest face, replacing the start of an ironic grin with a more serious stoicism.

"I wouldn't worry too much, Sister. Matty..." Ed searched for the right words, "...has a rather active imagination."

Benny scampered off the yellow-orange school bus in front of Whitney Elementary followed by several other kids, who chanted, "Benjamin-Benjamin! Benjamin-Benjamin! Benjamin-Benjamin! Is it your *first* name?! Is it your *last* name?!"

Benny spun back and shook his fist at them.

"Knock it off!"

They withdrew, knowing all too well that Benny would follow through on his threat if they didn't. Instead, they laughed at him and ran off while chanting even more loudly from a safer distance, "Benjamin-Benjamin, Benjamin-Benjamin...!"

Benny entered his classroom, tossed his lunch on the shelf above the coatrack, and began unzipping his coat. Halfway down, he realized he had completely forgotten to put his shirt on!

Oh no! It's still in the dryer at home!

He zipped the coat back up and dashed from the room.

Running as fast as he could, Benny backtracked the school bus's route, down one street and then another, and another. He looked both ways before carefully crossing a busy main intersection, raced down another very long block, and finally turned onto Oak Drive.

At the house, he bashed through the side gate and crawled into the dog-flap in the side door of the garage, retrieved a hidden house key from a jar on the tool bench, and opened the door between the garage and laundry room. He stripped off his coat, popped opened the dryer, slipped into his tee shirt, grabbed his coat, relocked the laundry room door, replaced the key, dove back out through the dog door, and dashed back out to the street.

"Benjamin Benjamin!"

Benny slowed his run to a trot in order to locate the voice.

"Come here, young man!"

It came from Mrs. Coe's front porch, where she leaned over the rail to glare at and coax him with an insistent finger.

He stopped on the sidewalk in front of her house, but didn't approach as requested.

"Benny's playin' hookie! Benny's playin' hookie!" her son, Ross, who stood next to her, taunted. Ross was still in his bathrobe.

"Shut up, Ross!" Benny yelled back.

"Why aren't you at school?" Mrs. Coe questioned.

"Why isn't *Ross* at school?!" Benny hollered back.

"Ross is sick today—*he* has an excuse. But we were talking about you, young man!"

"I can't talk right now, Mrs. Coe—you're gonna make me *late for school!*" Benny sassed back, as he dashed off.

22

Randy and Tony biked up to Carver Junior High together, parked and parted ways. Two grinning girls ran toward them. Randy grinned back. They called out, "Tony! Tony! Science class has a sub!"

Randy's face dropped.

All the girls at Carver thought Tony was cute, which was true, and all the girls thought Randy was weird, also true. Tony blithely moved on with his flock, abandoning his brother. Randy watched, envious of both his younger brother's adorers and Tony's ease with that fact.

Girls.

Randy reminded himself that once he became a famous film director, they'd all change their minds about him. His film class provided him with a camera and access to editing equipment. It was his favorite class *ever*.

He pulled the camera out of his book bag and looked through the view finder, pretending to film them in the hopes one of the girls might notice.

Tony halted at the door to his science class. He could hear a commotion inside. He crouched and swung the door open, allowing a paper wad from inside to fly past his head and out into the hallway. Tony entered with a dive to the floor in the middle of the yet-unsupervised class and into the no-man's-land of an already on-going paper-wad war. Scoping out the territory and who was on what side while arming himself with spent wads, he spotted Leslie Cooper cowering under her desk next to him. She was the prettiest girl in the school and, although all the other girls swooned over Tony, who could arguably be considered the best-looking boy, he had decided he only had eyes for Leslie.

Tony rolled a few paper wads to Leslie for protection.

She looked back, unimpressed by his act of gallantry.

Tony shrugged it off, gathered a new pile of wads for himself and stood in order to rapid-pelt the guys to his left—then, deciding to go rogue, he spun and shot the other direction to attack their opposition too, but his wad hit the balding man with a comb-over, tweed coat, and tie who just entered the classroom instead, right square in the forehead.

"Enough!" the man boomed, lofting a hand up for protection. "Settle down! Take your seats!"

Dozens of wads dropped to the floor as kids scrambled to their seats, discarding any evidence of participation.

The man waded through the flood of paper wads to the front of the room. He *squeeeaked* his name on to the chalkboard while informing, "I'm Mister Waxman. I'll be substituting for Miss Sewill today."

Mr. Waxman turned, lofted the trash bin next to Miss Sewill's desk, and motioned to Tony.

"You, what's your name?"

"Leslie Cooper," Tony answered mock-earnestly, glancing at Leslie and then the rest of his classmates.

"Well, Leslie," Mr. Waxman grinned, handing Tony the trash bin, "Clean up the floor and then take a seat **there**." He pointed to the stool in the front corner of the room.

His classmates "*Oooh*ed" and some of them snickered. Tony glanced at Leslie, who frowned at him and turned away, probably because he just stole her name.

"Any of you care to join him?" Mr. Waxman asked the class, pointedly.

The question was followed by dead silence and Mr. Waxman's momentarily triumphant smile.

Back at Whitney Elementary:

"...with liberty and justice for all," Benny's class intoned, finishing the Pledge of Allegiance.

From the back door of the classroom, Benny saw his chance. His classmates were taking their seats, providing cover as he stealthily slipped into the room to join them. His teacher, Mrs. Fowler, chalk in hand, faced the chalkboard with her back to him. He slipped his coat onto an empty hook and slinked to his desk in time to sit down with the rest. He struggled to catch his breath, smiling to himself.

She didn't see me. I did it.

Proud of himself, of his quick actions, his self-reliance, his ability to beat the odds and make it all the way home and back to class in the nick of time, he scanned the classroom. None of his classmates could have accomplished what he just had. His mom would have been proud of him. She would have said to him what she usually said when he figured a way out of a problem all on his own. "Look at that, Benny—you *fixed* it."

"*Benjamin Benjamin!*"

He glanced up from his thoughts to see Mrs. Fowler's furrowed brow glaring back at him.

The other kids laughed and a few whispered their taunt again, "Benjamin-Benjamin, Benjamin-Benjamin..."

Mrs. Fowler glanced at the clock and re-furrowed her brow at Benny.

Benny stood and answered, "Yes'm?"

"You're tardy."

"Well, I..."

"I want *no* excuses, young man. If I was grading you on punctuality, you'd get an eff!"

Benny glared defiantly back at her. His face reddened as she dismissed his morning's efforts without her even hearing him out. Without letting him *explain why.*

25

"Well?!" he exploded back, "If *I* was grading *you* on niceness, you'd get an **eff-minus!**"

The class gasped.

Mrs. Fowler's fresh stick of chalk shattered to pieces as it hit the floor.

At Jefferson High, a school bell marking the end of first period finished ringing. Ann entered the main hallway to join the swirling masses of her fellow students in transit. She meandered past and around and through them on her way to her next class, Driver's Training—with her handsome young instructor, Mr. Plummer—when the school's address system crackled and feed-backed to life with a tinny version of the school secretary, Mrs. Markey's, voice:

"Ann Benjamin, please report to the office. Ann Benjamin, to the office, please!"

"Rats," she thought, and with pinched brows, turned, and bucking the heavy flow of foot traffic, headed toward the school's main office.

Mrs. Markey's territory consisted of a waiting area with a stiff Naugahyde couch and access to a long hallway of individual administration offices behind it.

Ann approached Mrs. Markey, who was about to speak when Ann's senior counselor, D. J. Hammond, popped her head out of an office down the hall and motioned Ann to come with a, "Down here, Ann."

Mrs. Markey frowned from having her sense of order impinged upon.

"Thanks, Miz Markey," Ann said anyway, out of sympathy for the dour secretary.

Ann entered D. J.'s office.

D. J., or "Deej," as she preferred to be called by her students, was one of those exceptional people in education who seem to honestly care about each of her students. She was significantly younger than all the other administrative faculty and dressed in flared slacks rather than skirts most of the time. Her office smelled of incense and patchouli oil, was full of potted plants hung in macramé holders she knotted herself, and her walls were decorated with movie posters from *HELP!* and *The Umbrellas of Cherbourg.* Everyone considered her cool—especially the girls, and Ann found herself more often than not trying to dress like Deej.

Deej was modern and "liberated."

When kids had problems they couldn't talk to other adults about, they'd turn to Deej. And, for Ann, Deej had become almost a big-sister or surrogate mother.

Deej motioned to the phone lying off the cradle on her desk with a pink painted nail, giving her a knowing look.

"It's your father again."

Ann rolled her eyes back at Deej, and crossed to pick up the phone.

"Hi, Daddy. What... *What...?*"

Deej returned to her desk, sat, and began writing.

Ann miffed, "What'd he do *now?* ... But I'll miss my driver's ed class! ... We were going out in a real car today and... I know. ... *I know!* ... *Fine.* ... I'll take care of it. ... Okay. ... Bye," her voice dropped.

Deej exchanged a hall pass and a sympathetic look for the phone receiver.

"I'll let Mister Plummer know you've been excused."

On her way to the bike racks Ann spotted handsome Mr. Plummer lecturing her classmates in the parking lot next to a car with a "student driver" sign mounted atop it and grumbled. She then spotted Frank through the window

27

of Mr. Pratt's classroom. She waved and jumped up and down, trying to get Frank's attention, to let him know what was going on, but it was no use.

Whatever it was Frank was intent upon, it must have been one of his mean jokes, because that's all he favored lately. Ann gave up, cursed at him to herself, and stomped off to mount her bike.

Meanwhile inside the classroom, Frank sat, hands folded, pretending to listen to Mr. Pratt with a smirking, mock attentiveness.

Mr. Pratt sat snugly at his desk addressing his students.

"In short, due to your *dismal* test scores, only a few of you will progress to the next unit..."

He stood and lofted the pile of tests.

"...the rest will have to go back and try again."

A collective moan rose from the class as Mr. Pratt began handing back the graded and sorted tests to the front of each row of seats.

"It will be obvious by your scores which group to which you belong."

Mr. Pratt handed Frank back his test, marked with an A+.

"*Very* nice work, Frank. I especially like your essay."

"Thank you, sir."

Mr. Pratt addressed the whole class.

"I hope the rest of you will follow Frank's lead. As sophomores, college may seem a long way off, but negligence will always get you in the end," he pronounced, raising an emphatic finger before turning back to his desk, revealing the word "WIDE" imprinted on one of his ample butt cheeks in chalk and "LOAD" across the other.

The class erupted in a spontaneous burst of laughter.

As Mr. Pratt turned back to face the class, Frank swallowed his grin and pointed in mock-surprise to his teacher's rear end, causing Mr. Pratt to twist and pull on his trousers to see what was there, forcing him to walk in a circle. The class continued laughing as Mr. Pratt swatted pale clouds of yellow dust from his behind and inspected his chair to find the remains of the words written in reverse in chalk dust.

Ann parked her big bike in the racks of all the little bikes in front of Whitney Elementary School and entered the school's front office.

The office was airy and well-lit. The school was a year-new cinderblock building of modern flat roofs, floor to ceiling, clerestory, and jalousie windows, and globe pendant lamps, but the front office's basic arrangement was similar to Ann's older high school—a secretary's desk fronting a row of administrative offices behind.

Modernity could not improve upon some things, it seemed.

Sweet old Miss Kelly, the secretary Ann expected to see and who knew her well, wasn't behind her desk today though—this secretary was new. The hand-lettered cardboard name plaque on the desk read, "Mrs. Rynde."

Ann approached this stranger, who, after a quick glance up from her typing, continued to type without missing a stroke.

"Excuse me, Miz Rynde?" Ann interrupted.

Mrs. Rynde stopped in deliberately dramatic annoyance, breathed a sigh, pushed her horn-rimmed glasses up on her nose, and replied with a belabored, "Yes...?"

"I'm here about Benny Benjamin?"

"You're... his *mother?*"

"Our mother passed away. I'm his big sister. May I see him, please?"

Mrs. Rynde went back to typing.

"I'm sorry, I can't allow that. He's in the isolation room as punishment for insolence."

"Pardon...?"

"We require a *parent.*"

"*I'm* responsible for him," Ann bristled back, losing patience, "I was called by my father and *asked* to come here. I'd like to see my brother now, please!"

Mrs. Rynde stopped typing again, huffed anew, pursed her lips, and replied, "I'm sorry, Miss Benjamin, but school policy *clearly* requires..."

"Ann...?"

It was the principal, Mr. Specter, interrupting.

"Hi, Mister Specter," Ann sighed, relieved to see him. Mr. Specter had been one of her teachers back when she went to Whitney Elementary—before the new campus was built and he became principal.

"Your father called me to let me know you were coming." He turned to Mrs. Rynde. "I'll take it from here. Thank you, Missus Rynde."

"No trouble at all, sir," she replied to Mr. Specter, in a much softer tone and with a sweet smile.

Ann wanted so much to smack her silly.

They entered Mr. Specter's office and he closed the door, bidding Ann to sit across from his desk.

"Sorry about that," he apologized. "Our dear Miss Kelly finally retired. I'm not so sure we've found her replacement yet."

30

"It's okay," Ann replied with a chuckle, "I'm glad you interrupted me when you did though, or you may have had to send me to the isolation room with Benny."

He laughed.

"I'm really sorry about him," Ann continued. "I'll talk to him. It won't happen again."

Mr. Specter laughed again.

"This time he flunked Missus Fowler on 'niceness.' Just between you and me, I'd only give her a C minus myself."

Mr. Specter took on a more serious tone and expression.

"Ann, all of you Benjamin kids have been such exceptional students. So is Benny. His academic work is right at the top of his class, but he can't seem to control that temper of his. He's been having trouble with the other kids. I told your father and want to warn you too—there are laws concerning unsupervised children. Now, we're good here at Whitney, but if there's a problem elsewhere or at home and someone reports it...?"

Mr. Specter ran his hands through his hair and sighed.

"I really wouldn't want to see... anything happen to you kids."

His eyes met Ann's. She slowly nodded back to let him know she knew what he meant.

"We'll be very careful."

"Good!" he said in a positive tone, slapping his hands on his desk as he rose.

Ann stood too.

Mr. Specter looked her over and smiled.

"You've really grown into a beautiful young woman, Ann! Planning for college next year?"

"If we can afford it," she replied, crossing her fingers

and blushing at the compliment.

"Let me know if you need a recommendation."

He led her down the hall to a door marked "Isolation Room."

"He's right in there."

Mr. Specter turned and called out sternly, "Missus Rynde, would you step into my office for a moment please?"

"Certainly, Sir," she replied and clipped in.

Mr. Specter turned to Ann and winked at her as he ran a finger across his neck.

Ann walked a sullen Benny back toward his class. She stopped at a bench next to the empty playground near his classroom door.

"Wait. Sit with me for a sec, Benny. We need to talk."

He reluctantly sat and toed the ground, kicking at pebbles.

Ann leaned down but was unable to get Benny to make eye contact.

"Benny, look at me."

He scowled up.

"I didn't do anything wrong. She just wouldn't *listen*," he blurted, clenching his jaw. "I made it to class in time. I was *good*."

"It's not enough to be good," Ann sighed back. "We have to be better than all the other kids."

"That's not fair." He turned his attention back to the ground.

"No, it's *not* fair. Not fair at all. But people like Miz Fowler are watching us, they're waiting for us to screw up, so they can say the Benjamins can't take care of themselves anymore... and they'll... they'll *split us up*."

32

"So?"

"Benny! We're *family!* We have to stick together."

Benny glared back up to Ann and snapped, "You're going away to college."

That hit the mark, and it hurt. And she knew both why it hurt and why Benny had lobbed it at her: all of them missed their mom and the way she could make *everything* work, make *all* of them shine, make *each* of them feel special.

Mom wasn't here to see him through this. Ann was, and her mother made it clear on her death bed it was to be her responsibility to carry on in her place.

A rush of failure and helplessness swept Ann. She started to cry.

Benny took her hand.

"I'm sorry," he whispered. "I'll be good."

"You're good *already*," she returned, giving him a quick hug and adding, "I love you, Benny."

He half-hugged her back, then broke away.

"I gotta go," he mumbled back before dashing off to return to class.

Sisters Paula, Louise, and Martha floated about the tables during arts and crafts time at St. Helena's, peeling stubby crayons for and passing out fresh paper to their pre-school aged charges.

Due to the season, the theme of the day was "Halloween."

Matty Benjamin sat among them, scribbling away at his drawing and humming to himself. Art was Matty's place where he was in complete control—he could tell the story *he* wanted to tell, make the world look and act whatever way *he* wanted it to be. His world didn't have nuns in it or other stupid kids or any older brothers or bossy sister or any adults at all telling him what to do.

Sister Paula whooshed in theatrical astonishment and held up a drawing done by the shy little blonde girl with nose-freckles who only started coming to St. Helena's a few days earlier.

"Why, this is so lovely, Tina!" Sister Paula gushed. "Look, Sisters," she continued, motioning Sisters Louise and Martha to come look too.

Matty glanced over and saw that it was just a picture of a dumb old orange Jack-O-Lantern. Okay—it wasn't *totally* dumb. But it was... *boring*.

He sensed Sister Louise drifting his way and soon she hovered over his shoulder. He kept humming to himself and pretended to ignore her. He added some more green grass to his sketch.

It was a placid landscape of rolling hills and big, sturdy oak trees, topped with a cerulean blue sky full of puffy white clouds. He had used periwinkle at the bottoms of the clouds to shade them and give them dimension. It was a very well-drawn, pretty, and idyllic image. Matty had even added some colorful wildflowers here and there in the foreground.

He reached for the sepia crayon and began making rows of small brown squiggles near the base of one of the foreground hills when Sister Louise's hand snatched up the drawing.

"Sisters!" she exclaimed excitedly, and Sisters Paula and Martha floated over to join her. "Look at what Matty drew! Isn't it *lovely!*"

The nuns *ooh*ed and *aah*ed.

"*So* beautiful," Sister Martha gushed.

Sister Louise was pleased, and relieved. Considering all the severed heads and violent sketches Matty had done

34

during art-time lately, this one was pastoral and pleasant.

"But, what's... *this?*" Sister Louise asked, setting the drawing back in front of Matty and pointing to a dark, rocky tunnel at the base of the closest hill.

"A cave," Matty replied casually, as he continued adding more brown squiggles near its entrance.

"What's the cave for?" Sister Martha asked.

"That's where they put all the bodies," Matty replied.

The nuns' faces froze.

"And... *those...?*" Sister Paula asked with trepidation, pointing to the squiggles.

"Hungry worms."

The three sisters exchanged horrified looks and Sister Martha made the sign of the cross.

Back at Garfield Junior High, Tony was still seated on the stool-of-punishment in the front corner of his classroom. He'd been allowed to retrieve his science text, which he currently occupied himself with by drawing a flip-book of a rocket launch in its upper corner.

Their substitute teacher, Mr. Waxman, having been able to establish some order in Miss Sewell's class by making an example of Tony (who he still thought was named Leslie) had not yet caught onto the fact that all the other students had followed Tony's lead and had been exchanging names with each other all morning to deliberately confuse him, nor had he noticed that it was now about time for them to all start switching their names back. They had finished the day's chapter on basic chemistry and Mr. Waxman was plodding through the review questions at the end of it with the enthusiasm of a DMV agent reciting driver's license application instructions.

"The chemical formula of water is aiche-two-oh, which stands for..."

He scanned the rows of dull faces staring back at him while making his pregnant pause.

"...A: two oxygen atoms and one hydrogen atom; B: two hydrogen atoms and one oxygen atom; or C: two helium atoms and one osmium atom."

He looked up and was met *again* with a room full of unblinking, dull stares.

"*Anyone...?*"

Walt made the mistake of blinking.

"Keith, do you want to answer?" Mr. Waxman asked, pointing to him.

"I'm *Walt*," he replied.

"*I'm* Keith," Keith interjected.

"**Walt** then," Mr. Waxman corrected and sighed, "Which is it? A, B, or C?"

"What was the question?"

While Mr. Waxman droned a repeat of the question, Tony scanned the chalkboard where the formula for the day's lab experiment had been written out by Miss Sewell the night before. The first part required mixing sodium chloride—table salt, NaCl—with water.

Hmm...

Behind Mr. Waxman's back, Tony quietly tip-toed over, lofted the chalk eraser, and with a grin and a pantomime flourish, erased "Cl" from the formula before slipping back to his punishment stool.

"Walt, do you have the answer yet?" Mr. Waxman pressed.

"What are the choices again?" Walt asked with a deliberately puzzled look that made it clear to his classmates he was screwing with the sub.

"Ooooh! Oooooooh! *Ooooh!*" Tony hooted from his corner, holding his hand aloft, "I know! I know!"

Mr. Waxman, having lost patience with Walt and the rest of the deadpan class, turned back and, after a moment of deliberation, replied, "Very well, Leslie."

I'm Leslie," Leslie Cooper replied.

"Then who are *you?*" Mr. Waxman asked, his jaw clenched, the realization he had been *had* beginning to dawn.

"Tony Benjamin, sir," Tony replied, with as sincere a look of innocence as his handsome face could muster.

Mr. Waxman rolled his eyes and clipped, "Very well... *Tony*... If you answer correctly you may return to your seat."

"B: two hydrogen atoms and one oxygen atom, aiche-two-oh, water!" he perked.

"Right," Mr. Waxman sighed, relieved that at least one small thing went right this morning.

Tony zipped to his chair.

Mr. Waxman glanced at the clock and, realizing he was behind schedule said, "Okay, books away. Miss Sewell was kind enough to write out today's chemistry experiment on the chalkboard for us."

He crossed to a cupboard labeled, "Chemistry Supplies" and began extracting what was needed. With the cupboard door open and his view blocked, Tony frantically scribbled on a piece of paper—he tore the paper into strips and handed them to his fellow students in every direction.

He handed one to Leslie. She read it:

DUCK AND COVER!!!—pass it on

She gave Tony a confused look, but passed the note on.

By the time Mr. Waxman had all the supplies at the front worktable no notes were visible and the class looked keenly attentive.

He didn't really catch that their attention was fixed on Tony rather than him.

Mr. Waxman glanced at the first step in the formula on the chalkboard.

"First we make a solution of sodium and water... not clear how much sodium to use..."

Mr. Waxman used forceps to extract a small cube of sodium from several stored in a jar of kerosene, held it over a beaker half-full of water, and let it drop as Tony—and then every other student—dove under their desks.

Deej entered the Jefferson High teacher's lounge asking, "Did anyone else hear all those sirens?"

Mr. Pratt, who stood by the sink daubing his trousers with a damp cloth trying to remove the last of the chalk dust from his rear, huffed," It was probably *me* you heard. I swear, if something isn't done about this wave of vandalism..."

"It's the ghost of Billy Bobbs, back for revenge," Miss Espy, the art teacher and a free spirit explained, as if it was obvious to everyone.

"Elaine, please," Mr. Pratt scoffed, "No one knew the boy was anemic. It was merely a tragic coincidence he died in detention."

"Besides," Deej interjected with a smirk, "his ghost would have graduated two years ago. He's most likely off haunting the college of his choice by now."

"Go ahead and laugh at what you don't understand," Miss Espy sighed, sipping at her chamomile tea from her seat on the couch across the room.

The school principal seated next to her, Mr.

Bumsteader, folded his newspaper and set it on the coffee table with a narrowed sideways glance at Miss Espy.

"Itching powder on the toilet paper, archery targets that bleed, doors falling off their hinges?" he countered. "These are things we can all understand as student pranks, Elaine."

Mr. Pratt finished daubing himself. He crossed to the coffee urn followed by Deej with her cup. Mr. Bumsteader rose and grabbed his cup off the coffee table to cross and join the others around the urn as he continued.

"We all need to keep our eyes open. Be alert to anything suspicious. We need to catch this gang of pranksters before anything *really* serious happens."

He and Mr. Pratt both politely bid Deej to go first, so she put her cup under the coffee urn's spigot and turned it. Nothing came out. Mr. Bumsteader opened the lid and looked inside.

Deej looked inside the urn too. It appeared to be full of coffee.

But something was... *odd*.

Mr. Bumsteader lifted the urn and tilted it over the sink.

"What the...?"

A large, urn-shaped loaf of coffee-colored jello slurped neatly out to jiggle mockingly at them from the sink.

"Strong coffee," Deej giggled, but then, glancing over to see Mr. Bumsteader's less-than-amused reaction, she added, "Sorry."

Back at Garfield Junior High, each class had assembled in groups on the blacktop as a fire alarm continued to ring and firemen and policemen rushed about.

Mr. Waxman sat on a bench still testing his ears, surrounded by other concerned teachers.

Someone finally figured out how to turn off the alarm.

The fresh silence allowed the class a chance to give Tony guarded kudos from the boys and catch adoring smiles from the girls—even Leslie.

"Nice job, Benjamin!" Keith whispered. "But how did you know it would explode like that?"

"My brother, Randy, has a chemistry set," Tony confessed. "He did it in the kitchen sink and almost set our kitchen drapes on fire."

Walt laughed and pointed.

"Heh. Look at the cops!"

Several policemen dressed in gas masks and rubber gloves headed toward their classroom.

The kids all smirked and giggled.

Tony glanced at Leslie.

She smiled back and enticed him to come nearer with a dainty curling finger as she slipped to a spot a little way back from the clot of their classmates. Tony slowly sidled over, trying not to look too eager.

"Hi," Leslie cooed.

"Hi."

"Wanna go steady?" she asked, with an edge of aggressive shyness.

Tony shrugged, "'Kay."

Leslie opened her purse and took out a soft plastic troll doll with a long shock of purple hair. She handed it to him.

"For bravery," she explained.

40

"Thanks."

She waited for him to gift her something back, but being clueless to this whole dating-gifting protocol, he simply stood there with a blank stare, so she slipped away before the other girls saw them together.

Tony shoved the troll doll into his pocket before the other boys could see it.

He and his classmates laughed anew at the policemen in their masks and gloves as one of them carried the rest of the jar of sodium out in front of himself with tongs as if it too would spontaneously explode.

Tony scanned and saw Randy grouped with his class. Randy saw him too and, knowing this had to be his work, gave him a proud grin and a thumbs-up.

Chapter Three

Functional Chaos

A neat-freak would manifest a mental breakdown if forced to enter and navigate the Benjamin household this particular afternoon. Cardboard boxes and a roll of aluminum foil looked to have done battle, cut each other to ribbons, and both lost a war in the living room; the only survivor being Benny's robot Halloween costume.

Sprawled on the floor in front of a blaring black & white TV airing *To Tell the Truth*, Randy attempted to pose and direct his pet rats while filming them with the school's movie camera.

"Look mean!" he ordered, gritting his teeth and growling at them. "You're evil devil spawn!"

The rats just continued sniffing around on the floor for dropped crumbs and being rats rather than actors.

His younger brother Tony, seated on an ottoman next to him, watched the TV while sorting through a cardboard box full of old Halloween masks and twiddling with his newly-acquired troll doll by swinging it around in tight circles by its long shock of hair.

Ann had her butt perched on the edge of the couch with a foot propped up on the coffee table and cotton balls between each toe, carefully painting her nails Stormy Pink: the same shade of pink she had seen Deej wearing.

This same lover of the orderly might also assume these unsupervised children were neglected. They would only see the disarray of floors strewn with paper, stray cotton balls, used plates full of cookie crumbs, moist milk glasses imprinting new rings on the furniture, and windows

43

smeared with pet-spittle. They wouldn't realize that this wasn't all that far removed from life in the Benjamin home before their mother had died. To the kids, this was situation: normal.

Somehow Ellen managed to make it all work and keep any mess looking rational and creative rather than chaotic. But without her influence to give it a clear structure, the jury was out.

Benny entered the kitchen dragging the top half of his foil and cardboard construction in search of something dangerously sharp to punch eyeholes in it. Frank stood at the kitchen table fiddling with a blue-flamed propane torch, wires, and some glass tubing.

"Waddaya doin'?" Benny asked.

"Building a laser. Waddaya doin'?" Frank mocked back.

Benny held up his construction.

"Robot," he answered.

Frank nodded.

"What's a *laser?*" Benny asked.

"It's like a ray gun."

"Good. I need a ray gun for my costume. So I can kill Ross Coe with it."

Frank stopped what he was doing to look at Benny's robot with uncharacteristic admiration and a laugh.

"How about blinking lights instead?" Frank offered, feeling generous and digging around in his box of electronic parts to extract an old string of miniature twinkle lights. "They won't kill anybody, but they'll look pretty cool."

"'Kay. But you can't do it for me. I have to do everything myself. It's the rules."

Back in the living room, Chocolate-Drop, Randy's black and white rat, scampered over to Tony while Tony tried on and stacked plastic Halloween masks. When he wasn't looking it grabbed his troll doll in its teeth by the hair.

"Yes!" Randy exulted as he filmed the action with his movie camera.

"Oh no!!! It's radiation rat! *Aaaaahhhhh!!!* Help! Help *meeee*...!" Randy vamped as Chocolate-Drop dragged the troll away. Mucklethorpe, Randy's tan and white rat, sniffed his way over to sink his teeth into one of the troll's feet.

A rat tug of war ensued.

"Argh! They've multiplied!!! They're tearing me in two!"

Tony set down his mask and rolled onto his belly on the ottoman to watch and laugh along.

A very interested cat meow penetrated the sliding glass doors to the back yard, where Mommacat and several of her current kittens eyed the rats, their many heads darting back and forth in perfect sync as they followed the rats' movements about the floor.

Randy shifted the camera to the cats.

"Fortunately, our force field keeps out the even more horrifying army of giant radioactive cat mutants."

"Ooh, a force field," Tony smirked.

From across the room Ann snickered out, "You're such a goof," while switching feet to begin painting the next batch of cotton-balled toes.

"No, I'm not," Randy smirked back, "I'm a movie director."

"Same thing," Ann shot back.

"Don't interrupt me while I'm filming," Randy retorted.

45

Frank and Benny entered with Frank carrying Benny's robot top for him.

"Filming what?" Frank laughed, "Being a spaz?"

"No, my movie for my class final: Killer Rats from Outer Space."

Benny raised his arms and Frank helped place the robot costume over his head.

"Watch this," Frank grinned. "Presenting... laser robot!"

"I did it myself!" Benny's muffled voice hollered from inside.

Frank flipped a switch on the front of the costume. A grid-like array of blinking lights lit up and began randomly flashing across the robot's chest.

Everyone *oohe*d and *aahe*d their approval, with Randy adding, "Wow, Benny! Can I use this in my movie?"

Ann rolled her eyes and sniffed derisively.

"What's it look like? What's it look like?" Benny called from inside, hopping up and down in excitement. The robot's eyes were still uncut.

Frank had a pencil in hand. He placed a heavy hand on Benny-the-Robot's box head to steady it.

"Hold still a minute so I can mark your eyeholes. Then you'll be able to see for yourself."

"***NO DON'T!!!*** I have to do it myself!" Benny protested.

The phone rang. Ann replaced the long brush cap into her jar of polish and leapt to her cotton-balled, wet-nailed feet, with toes curled skyward, to quickly hobble on her heels to the kitchen and answer it.

"Hello? Oh, hi, Daddy... Uh-huh."

She cradled the phone with a shoulder and carefully extended a wet-nailed hand, opened the refrigerator, extracted the casserole, removed the Saran Wrap, slid it into the oven, and turned the oven to 350°.

"Yes—dinner is in the oven…"

She glanced at the clock, reconsidered, and turned the oven temperature knob up to 475°, then hobbled back to the doorway to shush her brothers and get their attention.

"Our chores…? We're doing them now. The teevee…?" She waved madly with her free arm toward Randy. Randy leapt at the TV and clicked it off.

"No, it's off," Ann continued. There was a brief pause as she listened, and her brothers all cocked their ears, trying to pick up on what was being said.

"Wait… hold on," Ann interjected, "Who's that talking? *Sister Martha?* You're at **Saint Helena's already?**"

She shot a panicked look at her brothers.

"Home in **ten minutes?**"

Benny's muffled grunts and gasps drew attention back to him. His lights fritzed out and puffs of smoke were seeping from the top of the robot's head.

"Uh-oh," Frank whispered, "Benny must have crossed some wires!"

"Okay, bye, Daddy," Ann finished, hanging up the phone, followed immediately by announcing, "**Martial law!!!**"

An actual sparking flame shot out the front of Benny's costume and Ann squealed. Frank batted it out while blind Benny thrashed about with muffled screams from within.

Frank crossed to the sliding glass doors to vent the smoke, letting all the cats in.

"NO, FRANK!!! *MY RATS ARE OUT!!!*"

Randy chased after his rats while shooing the cats away from them.

Benny continued thrashing around blindly in circles, yelling, "Help! Get me outta here!"

Tony leapt to Benny's rescue, but Benny kept inadvertently batting him back.

Chaos bounded in, knocked Benny over, and took to chasing Randy, the cats, and the rats around the house.

Frank repeated the cry, **"Martial law, guys!"** as he stood momentarily immobilized, tearing at his hair, before dashing to the garage to retrieve the push broom and return to the living room to furiously shove all the mess of foil and cardboard and troll doll and school texts and magazines and cotton balls and masks and papers into a huge pile.

Meanwhile, Randy captured his rats and safely latched them back in their cage. He then retrieved the vacuum cleaner from the hall closet, but rather than using it to vacuum, he switched the hose from the intake to the exhaust and set it to blowing cool air at the backside of the TV.

After quickly pondering the possibilities, Frank finally shove-shove-shoved the great pile of living room mess into the front hall closet Randy had left open.

Ann dashed on her thumping heels back to the kitchen. She grabbed the dish rag and wiped the counter crumbs onto the floor with instant regret as she looked down to see her still freshly painted toes now coated in crumbs. Not allowing herself even time to moan, she soaped up the rag and went at the morning dishes in a mechanical frenzy, soaping, rinsing, and racking them up at record speed. Finishing, she rinsed her hands clean and, hesitating, held them up.

Her fingernails were now a mottled mess. She glanced at the racked dishes to see little specks of Stormy Pink everywhere.

"*Aaaarrrrggh!!!*" She groaned, but there was no

time to waste on regrets or a redo. She grabbed a broom from the kitchen closet and swept the dirt and crumbs from the floor into the still-open closet only to spin and see Chaos seated across the room next to a puddle of his own pee, wagging his tail proudly.

"Thanks, Chaos," she sighed, grabbing a wad of paper towels, "Thanks, a lot."

After flailing on the floor like an upturned turtle, Tony finally got Benny free of his costume with a lot of tugging on his feet.

"*Air...*" Benny wheezed, when his head emerged.

"No time!" Tony snapped back, "Get the other side!"

The two turned Benny's costume upside down to use like a bucket and collected kittens in it.

Feeling they finally had captured them all, they tipped the costume, dumping them outside, and closed the sliding door.

Ann dashed in, dragging Chaos by the collar, reopened the sliding door again to put him out, and in the process allowed several of the eager kittens back in.

"ANN!!!" Tony and Benny screamed.

"Sorry! *Sorry!*" she shot back, as all three of them chased kittens again.

Upstairs, in Tony, Benny, and Matty's bedroom, Frank used his handy push broom method to shove the last of his younger brothers' clothes, toys, books, and junk under Tony's bed. The mattresses of both Tony's bed and Benny's lower bunk bulged up a bit from all the junk piled beneath them. In order to hold back the piles, Frank pulled their bedspreads taut and locked their corners under the bottoms of the bed legs to hide and keep everything in place before moving on.

49

Meanwhile, Randy was in his and Frank's bedroom. The floor was strewn with dirty clothes, comics, and other junk. He opened the closet wide and leaned over like a football center to hike everything on the floor between his legs into it.

Ann burst into her own bedroom, emptied her trash bin into her bottom desk drawer, smoothed and shaped her bedspread over her unmade bed, and tossed everything out of place into her closet.

The Benjamin kids all did one last gleaning through the house, gathering armloads and bits of anything still out of place while Randy pursued one last stray kitten.

Just as Randy nabbed the evasive little feline and turned off the vacuum, they all froze.

It was the sound of the station wagon pulling into the driveway.

"*Aaaaaaaahhh!!!*" they all wailed as they made their final dashes.

When Ed and Matty entered the quiet house, Ed found his children calmly seated and sprawled about the living room as if posing for a *Life* magazine photo spread. Ann, tucked into one corner of the couch, read her history text while Tony, seated on the floor at the coffee table beside her, wrote an essay. Randy sprawled on floor exactly as he was all afternoon, but this time with an open textbook in front of him instead of his rats and camera.

Benny had his costume perched neatly on the hearth, carefully marking where to the cut the eyeholes.

"Hi, Dad," they all chirped.

Frank came around the corner carrying a laundry basket full of clean clothes from the dryer.

"Oh. Hi, Dad," he perked too, as if he wasn't expecting to see him, "Just going up to fold the last of these," he explained as he hopped up the stairs with the basket and a smile.

Ed's eyes darted to and fro, like a novelty cat clock.

Not that he didn't trust his kids, but yeah... *he didn't trust them.*

"Everything... *okay?*" he asked, stepping slowly into the living room, still glancing about for any telltale signs of something amiss.

"Yup," Randy tossed back, not looking up from his text.

Ed crossed to the TV. He placed a hand on it. It was cool to the touch.

Randy rolled on his side to look up at his dad, smiling innocently.

Matty crossed to Ann and, seeing her mottled fingernails, asked, "What happened to your...?"

"Quiet, Matty," Ann whispered back with a glare, slipping her hands under her thighs.

Ed continued his inspection into the kitchen with all the kids shadowing him from a safe distance.

Ed could smell the casserole cooking, the dishes were washed, the counters were clear and clean, and the floor, swept.

Matty wandered over to climb the kitchen drawers and extract Lugee from its potted plant on the windowsill. He followed his father upstairs for the continued inspection carrying the slug.

Ed stepped into the younger boys' room. Matty's

51

eyes popped. He was surprised to see the completely clear floor and, wondering where all their junk went, started to tug at Tony's taut bedspread until Benny kicked him.

Ed glanced into Frank and Randy's room. As it appeared to be in tidy order too, he shut the door and continued on before the latch on their closet gave under stress and a pile of mess spilled out.

Ed finished in Ann's room. He entered to give it a full 180° turn, lingering long enough to glance into her trash bin and notice it had been emptied.

Ann smiled sweetly at him.

Back in the kitchen, Ann helped her brothers set the table.

Matty returned Lugee to its potted plant and washed his hands. He noticed the pink specks all over the sink and the dishes. He decided he liked them. He climbed down and looked over to watch in fascination as a sinuous thread of smoke started seeping from one corner of the oven door.

Ed observed his smiling kids and allowed himself to smile back, feeling relieved.

Well," Ed announced, as if reading a trial verdict, "You kids surprised me. A little shabby here and there, but all and all..."

He was interrupted by a muffled, "Mew."

"What was that?"

The kids froze. Ed looked at Matty.

Matty shrugged.

"Mew."

And... another forlorn, "Mew," followed as Ed sussed out the source of the sound—the front hall closet—while each of his kids tip-toed silently away in different directions.

He opened the door.

A massive mound of mess blew out to half bury Ed, as if he had just popped opened a giant tube of Pillsbury biscuit dough.

The trapped kitten hissed and skittered out between his legs, startling him.

Ed spun to confront his kids—but they had all magically vanished.

"Rrright," he growled.

Ed bolted through the house in search of them and as he searched, every closet revealed even more hidden mess. Each kid dodged from hiding place to hiding place and room to room, staying just out of reach, successfully evading him. Ed grew angrier and more frustrated, ranting and cursing at each, "Come back here! Dammit, Frank, *don't you run from me!!!* Benny, get over here this instant! There's **hell** to pay!!!"

Mrs. Coe hosed her front walkway while listening to the yelling, banging, screaming, swearing, crying, and commotion emanating from the Benjamin house next door.

Old Mr. and Mrs. Winter from down at the far end of the block were out for their usual evening stroll.

"Sounds like the Benjamins are at it again," Mr. Winter remarked with a sigh, knitting his ample gray brows at both his wife and Mrs. Coe.

"He must be a *monster*," Mrs. Winter replied, shaking her head. "Yelling at those poor, *sweet*, motherless children like that."

"Someone ought to *do* something about that family,"

Mrs. Coe snapped back with a scowl as she turned her hose on Mommacat, who was about to slink into her yard.

"...in our bounty through Christ our Lord. Amen," Ed said, finishing grace.

"Amen," the kids each whispered, adding their own silent prayers to God and crossing themselves.

In the center of the table sat the charred tuna-noodle casserole, still smoldering.

Ed scanned the table: Ann, Benny, and Matty all had red faces from crying, Frank and Tony wouldn't make eye contact with him. Oddly, Randy was grinning off into space, likely his way of covering his hurt?

How can I make this work, Ed wondered?

He had always dealt out the discipline, sure, but Ellen had written the child-rearing manual. And the truth was, when she had been around, there was never much need to punish or scold these kids. The other truth was: these were *her* kids, not *his* kids.

She had made it too easy for him to forget they were his responsibility too when she was alive because she did such a good job handling them all on her own. She made it easy for him to ignore them. This realization made him mad at her and blame her for his current feelings of incompetence, but it also felt very wrong to think this, to blame her, and he didn't want to be angry with her or think ill of her.

Well, they are my kids, he reminded himself.

The whole chain of thought was too painful, so he abandoned it.

It was replaced with the realization of how much he

had neglected them all: her, the kids, his entire home life.

He couldn't face it. It all hurt far too much. So, he buried these thoughts too.

"You *cooked* it, you *eat* it," was the best punishment he could come up with at the moment, as he excavated and doled out square chunks of the blackened clot that was dinner onto each plate.

Randy braved a bite.

"Crunchy," he decided.

The rest of the kids followed suit in an otherwise quiet chorus of crunching.

The phone rang.

Both Ann and Frank leapt up in unison, crying, "I'll get it!"

Ed rose and jerked up an insistent palm to stop them.

"*I'll* get it—you eat," he commanded. They slumped back to their chairs and returned to choking down the remains of their tuna-noodle briquettes.

"Hello?" Ed answered, "Yes, good evening, Miss Southern—yes, of course, I'm sorry... *Sabrina.* Thank you for returning my call. You looked over the specs I sent you? No problem. *That much?* Really?! Well, *good* then—good! Yes, let's meet... lunch tomorrow would be great. Thank you. Yes. Bye now."

Ed hung up using a finger to depress the receiver hook while rubbing his forehead with the earpiece end of the receiver, lost in thought.

The kids exchanged curious glances.

"Daddy...?" Ann asked, hesitantly. "What was *that* all about? Who's Miss Southern?"

"Sabrina," Randy corrected.

"A realtor," Ed replied. "I'm selling the house. We're

55

gonna move."

The quiet pall on the room instantly vanished, to be replaced with a noisy verbal firing squad:

"Move?! We *can't* move!" Ann shouted, standing.

"You mean *now*?! To *where*?!" Frank questioned, approaching him.

"Will I get to change schools?!" Benny asked, scrambling over to tug on his dad's pant leg.

Ann glanced at Benny, then back at her dad," We **can't** change schools! It's my senior year!"

"If the yard's bigger, can we get another dog?" Tony prodded. "A *good* dog?"

"If we're movin', I want my own room then!" Frank demanded, stepping closer.

"Me too!" Randy chimed, meeting him.

"Me **three**!!!" Benny finished, pushing in front of the other two.

"And a pool!" Tony added, while tugging his dad's sleeve, "Get one with a pool!"

"Lugee likes it here!" Matty cried.

Ed stopped rubbing his forehead with the phone receiver and started banging his head with it instead.

"You're not saying anything, Daddy!" Ann groused, getting right up in his face.

"*SHUT UP!*" Ed hollered, "All of you!"

The kids all instantly retreated beyond his reach and went mute.

Ed hung up the receiver. He pointed to the table and they slumped to their seats, patiently waiting while Ed returned to his.

He sat.

"Look," Ed finally responded, with a sigh. "Since

your mother died... well... we haven't been doing all that *well* here. I think we need a change. A fresh start."

Ann and Frank exchanged concerned looks.

"There are too many... *memories* here," Ed continued, trailing off, lost in thought, staring at his own charred dinner.

He finally looked up at his kids.

"I won't discuss it further, and that's final. It's *my* decision to make, *not* yours. Now button up and eat your dinner."

"But... this is our *home*," Ann mumbled, mostly to herself.

"Ann..." Ed's reprimand was interrupted by Randy's crunching.

Everyone looked at Randy.

"What?" Randy responded, continuing to crunch down a second crisp, casserole briquette. "I kinda like this! It's... tuna-noodle jerky."

Chapter Four

Treat or Trickery

Ed's alarm clock rang and his big feet hit the floor—he stomped down the ice-cold upstairs hallway in his robe to turn up the thermostat and pound a fist twice on each door he passed to bark, "Frank! Randy! Reveille!"

"Tony! Benny! Matty! Up and at 'em!"

He rapped with his knuckles on Ann's door.

"Annie! Time to get up!"

Benny was up already and dressed in blue pants and an almost-matching long-sleeved blue tee shirt. He eyed his robot costume with pride. Wearing all blue under the foil suit was Matty's suggestion and it was a pretty good one, as the blue reflected in the foil and helped him look more metallic. Benny had even glued foil to his old pair of sneakers. With these final touches and having a costume with real blinking lights, he was sure to win.

Ann ignored her father's raps while rereading the several pages she had written in her diary the night before—about her dad wanting to ruin everything and sell their home and move them all to God-knows-where. Getting it on paper didn't help. She was still angry about it.

She grabbed her pen and continued to add some fresh morning rants:

> Dad doesn't listen to me. None of them ever
> listen to me. Just because I'm a girl. It
> doesn't matter that I'm oldest—except

when Dad wants to blame someone! Then it's all, "You're the oldest!" It makes no sense.

Momma made me responsible for them. I have to keep trying. I don't have a choice. It's my job to tell them what I think and keep the family together.

And now he wants to sell the house?! Our home?! Over my dead body he will!

Randy preened before the bathroom mirror looking cleaner and tidier than usual. He rubbed some Brylcreem in his hair and then combed it neatly into place.

He smiled, revealing plastic vampire teeth.

Down in the kitchen, Matty did *his* chores—he switched Lugee into a fresh potted plant.

Upstairs, Frank waited until he was sure Ann was in the bathroom to sneak into her room to borrow her sophomore yearbook off her bookshelf. He stuffed it into his school bag and slipped out.

Breakfasts today for Benny, Matty, and Tony were pre-packaged small, individual Kellogg's Variety-Pack cereal boxes.

From upstairs they heard their dad yell, "Frank...?!"

Benny very carefully cut and tidily folded back doors in the front of his mini box of Corn Pops, as per the instructions on the box, and poured milk into it, only to have the buoyant Pops float out and roll every which way across the table.

"Noooo...!" he protested, but his Corn Pops didn't obey.

Ed popped his head into the kitchen.

"Have any of you seen your brother, Frank?" Ed asked.

The three boys glanced at each other and pantomimed back "See No Evil, Hear No Evil, Speak No Evil" poses.

"I'm raising a pack of monkeys," Ed grumbled.

The *scree-scree-scree* of the Jefferson High School janitor's cart faded around a corner. Frank emerged from behind the mock orange and once again popped the lock.

He slipped quietly into Miss Espy's pitch-dark art classroom. He plugged in and wheeled an opaque projector from the corner of the room to the center to aim it carefully at the big chalkboard in the front of the room.

He pulled out Ann's old yearbook and flipped open the full-page dedication to Billy Bobbs, the poor kid who had died while doing detention a couple years back.

Frank slipped the photo of Billy under the projector lenses and clicked it on, focusing the image of the dead kid's face in the center of the chalkboard.

Frank extracted a small paintbrush and a bottle of clear solution from his jacket pocket.

Matty and the rest of the children at Saint Helena's day care cannibalized the pile of supplies and art materials the sisters had set out on the large arts and crafts table. Today's activity was to make their own Halloween costumes from the paper bags, pipe cleaners, construction paper, glue, crayons, paper plates, glitter, and whatever else the sisters could scrounge up, and then to write a poem about their costume to share with the group.

Sister Martha, who was supervising arts and crafts, returned from the convent's kitchen with a roll of Saran Wrap—a special request from Matty.

"Here we are, Matthew," she said, holding up the boxed roll.

"Thank you, Sister Martha."

She pulled out a short six inches of the clear wrap.

"Will this do?" she offered

Matty shook his head. "No."

She extracted six more inches.

"This?" she offered hopefully.

"No."

"How much do you need, Matthew?

"Enough."

"Enough, huh?" she replied with a slight air of exasperation.

"Yup."

She sighed, "Here, I'll hold the box and you pull out as much as you'll need."

Matty gripped both corners of the clinging Saran and backed away from Sister Martha. Three feet—six feet—twelve feet—he stopped.

Sister Martha tore her end free for him.

"My!" she whooshed. "Now I'm *very* curious what you have planned for that."

Matty carefully took his end to the table where he was working and scotch taped it securely to the bottom front of his grocery bag costume. He had already carefully scissored out a face hole above where he taped the Saran

62

and had constructed two pipe-cleaner antennae topped by small balloons with pupils drawn on them in felt marker to create eyeballs on the top of his head.

His costume now complete, Matty put the bag over his head and pulled it down to cover most of his arms as well. He stepped over the long sheet of Saran wrap so that it trailed back between his legs and then he ever-so-slowly walked bow-legged to join the other children already sitting in the reading circle.

Sister Martha took the adult-sized chair in front.

"Children, quiet please. We are all ready to start. Gloria, why don't you go first? Come up here and tell us what you are and then read us your poem."

Gloria, one of the older kids in the group, sprang to the front. She had cut one cup out of a cardboard egg carton and painted a nose on it, added pipe cleaner whiskers, and a rubber band so she could wear it over her own nose. She had added pointy black construction paper ears to her violet plastic headband.

She unfurled her paper as if she was about to read a grand proclamation, and cleared her throat.

> *"I'm a cat.*
> *Other kids are this or that,*
> *but I'm a cat."*

"Thank you, Gloria," Sister Martha chuckled, "that was very direct."

Gloria returned to her seat.

Sister Martha scanned the row of children. Matty's curious-looking costume got the better of her.

"Matthew, why don't you go next?"

Unable to use his arms, Matty carefully rose from his chair and came forward very slowly, with his balloon-eyed antennae bobbing and googling around goofily, being careful to circle around the chairs so the Saran Wrap trailed back between his legs.

"Matthew? What *are* you?" Sister Martha inquired.

"I'm a slug."

Some of the other kids giggled and Gloria let out a curt, "Eeuw," but Sister Martha shushed them all.

"I see, a slug," Sister Martha replied, trying not to laugh too. "So, have you written a poem, Mr. Slug?"

"Slugs can't write," Matty explained.

Sister Martha nodded. "That's very true, Matthew."

"So I memorized it," he continued.

Sisters Louise and Paula entered, and Sister Martha motioned them to join her.

"The children are reciting their poems," she told them. "As you can see, Matthew is a slug."

The sisters' eyes grew wide and they tried to suppress giggles. Sister Martha nodded toward the googly-eyed Matty. "Go ahead, Matthew."

> *"A slug is slow*
> *A butterfly sails*
> *But only the slug*
> *Leaves shiny trails."*

The Sisters' giggles morphed into smiles hearing Matty's insightful poem.

"Yes, they do," Sister Paula agreed, "They certainly do. Thank you, Matthew. That was a very thoughtful poem and you make a wonderful slug."

He looked up wide-eyed with his Renaissance-cherub face framed in brown paper, balloon-eyes still wobbling around sillily over his head. He smiled sweetly back at the three sisters.

Adorable was Matty's magical power, to turn on or off at will, and the sisters were defenseless.

Sister Paula sighed and Sister Martha touched his

64

paper-wrapped shoulder affectionately, then led him back
to his seat, being careful not to step on his slime trail.

In the Garfield Junior High cafeteria, Tony sat eating
his sack lunch, Leslie Cooper at his side, and surrounded by
a corona of giggling girls. Leslie pulled an Oreo from her
sack lunch.

"Would you like a cookie?" she offered,

The rest of the girls, vying for his attention, would
not be outdone.

"Have a Twinkie," offered Susanne Barker, a cute
red head. A brownie appeared, and then one of the little
cafeteria ice cream cups with its wooden spoon was set in
front of him.

"Wow, thanks," Tony responded, grinning at each,
happily puzzled by all the attention.

Only last year, when they were all still at Whitney
Elementary, none of the girls wanted to be anywhere
near him, or any of the other boys for that matter. Now,
Tony's twelve year old wavy brown hair, naturally athletic
body, easy smile, and pool-blue eyes translated into being
considered "cute"—and being offered free desserts?

"Cool!"

Leslie glowered at the other girls and stuck out her
tongue at Susanne, who was runner-up for cutest girl in the
school, second only to Leslie.

Randy came over to stand next to Tony. Tony grinned
up at his older brother.

"Hey, Randy, want some of my desserts?" he offered,
bragging.

"Noooo," Randy cried, oozing catsup from between

his vampire teeth to drip across the table, "I seek... *bloooood!!!*"

The girls all shrieked, "Eeeeewww! Gross!" and scattered while Randy taunted them.

"Blood, I want fresh blood!"

"Tony! Make him stop!" cried Leslie.

Tony just laughed, thinking Randy hilarious.

"Blood!"

Leslie Cooper snatched back her Oreo cookie.

"Your brother's too gross, and you don't care," she complained, "I don't wanna be your girlfriend anymore. Gimme back my troll!"

"M'Kay," Tony replied with a shrug. He dug the troll doll out of his pocket, picked some lint off of it, and handed it back to her.

She examined it closely and noticed tiny chew marks and a few missing toes.

"What did you *do* to it?!" She cried, "Try to *eat* it?!"

"No, my rats did," Randy smirked, as he wiped his mouth clear with a napkin and sucked his plastic teeth clean before removing them.

"*Eeeeuww!!!*" she squealed, tossing the troll doll into Tony's lap. "I don't want it anymore. Ick! You *ruined* it! I *hate* you, Tony Benjamin!"

Leslie rushed off to go wash her hands.

Randy looked at Tony.

"Sorry."

"*Pshhh*—I don't care," Tony shrugged, picking up the troll doll and thinking it was pretty cool after all, now that it had scars.

After lunch and a very unproductive math time, Benny and his classmates, indeed all of Whitney Elementary, were allowed to don their Halloween costumes and spend the rest of the afternoon having class parties, ending with a big, school-wide costume parade where they all marched around the schoolyard blacktop to tunes like *The Monster Mash*, the theme song from *The Addams Family*, Billy Buchanan's *Beware*, *Graveyard Rock*, and other ghostly music and sounds.

It was difficult to walk in the foil-covered cardboard tubes Benny had fashioned for his legs and arms, and it was utterly impossible for him to sit down once in costume, so he was already pretty tired before the parade even started. He had successfully fixed his wiring so the costume lit up perfectly, but out in the sunlight no one could really tell it was lit.

Shoot.

Benny felt beads of sweat traveling down his forehead and back. A drip hung from his nose but he was unable to do anything other than endure it. He hadn't realized that wrapping himself in aluminum foil and marching around the blacktop would bake him like a potato. It would all be worth it in the end, he reassured himself. Most of the other kids were wearing either store bought costumes or ones their mothers had sewn for them.

They're all disqualified.

Of the few self-made ones, Benny knew his was the best by far. They weren't going to give the prize to a simple, stupid sheet ghost or hobo. Nope. This year's trophy for Best Costume was his.

He jiggled his head to force the drop of sweat off his nose while keeping up his practiced robot walk—stiff and mechanical, with an occasional rotation at his waist.

The heavy smell of sweat-moistened cardboard and his deviled-ham-sandwich and barbequed-potato-chips breath was nauseating and made him wish he had thought

67

ahead to design air holes or a mouth grille into the costume.

The music mercifully ended and the children were corralled into class groups on the lawn. Mr. Specter, dressed as Captain Hook, stepped up to a microphone.

"Okay, all you ghosts and goblins! Let's all settle down, please," he ordered, fighting feedback. "Go ahead and sit down in your class groups. Our creeeeepy panel of judges has reached their decisions and we are ready to give out the awards."

All the kids sat but Benny, because he couldn't.

"Sit down, Benjamin," Mrs. Fowler scolded.

"I can't!" he groused back in a muffle.

Fortunately, Mrs. Fowler didn't press the issue and let him remain standing—this was her in a festive mood.

Mr. Specter continued pattering on, passing out the various small plastic trophies, followed by applause, for several age groups and categories. Most Historic was won by a sixth-grade girl who came as a post-guillotined Marie Antoinette—she tossed her head in the air with joy at winning. Scariest went to another sixth-grade boy who had knives, swords, and a red-hot poker with the tip painted with fluorescent orange paint jammed into and through him, with an axe embedded in his head, and lots of fake blood. Funniest went to a cute little kindergartener who simply put his store-bought Fred Flintstone costume and mask on backward and then walked everywhere backward.

He finally got to the main award— a bigger plastic trophy for "Best Costume." He repeated the criterion for winning the award as his build-up: you had to have made the costume all yourself, no help from others, and not store bought.

Mr. Specter finished with, "...and so, Whitney Elementary School is proud to present this year's Halloween trophy for Best Costume to..."

Benny held his breath.

68

"...Pamela Love!"

There was a round of applause as Pamela, dressed as a fairy princess, with an elaborately sequined dress, bejeweled cellulose crown, glittery tulle and wire wings, and a silver wand topped with a glittered starburst flitted up to join Mr. Specter, grinning and curtsying.

Benny struggled to get out of his costume, shaking off the arm tubes. Two of his classmates helped him pull off the top and he could then remove the leg tubes, finally able to wipe the sweat—now mixed with the beginnings of angry tears—from his eyes as he watched Mr. Specter hand Pamela *his* trophy.

"It's a beautiful costume, Pamela. Did you make *all* of this yourself?!" Mr. Specter complimented, with a wink.

"Well," Pamela blushed, "My mom helped me a *little*."

Pamela stepped back to her class group with another round of applause.

But Benny wasn't clapping.

"Okay, children," Mr. Specter continued, "Quiet, please! Let's head back to your classes in an orderly fashion, and may all of you have a very Happy Halloween!"

Benny stared down at his costume. His losing costume. The lights were still twinkling at him, mocking him.

He switched them off.

"The rules were you make it *yourself*," he grumbled, stuffing all the limb tubes inside and gripping the lower edge of his costume top to drag it back to class.

Mrs. Fowler turned to Benny.

"What did you say?" she asked him.

Benny shot her a mute glower.

"Perhaps you'd like to share what you said with the

69

rest of the class?"

"I said, the rules were you make your costume *yourself—no help!*" he growled back. "She *cheated.*"

His classmates circled, hoping for some good fireworks.

"Well, Benjamin," Mrs. Fowler replied, looking at his costume, especially noting the lights. "You obviously had help crafting yours. We should not accuse others of our own faults."

"I ***did*** make it all myself!"

"We don't *lie* in this school, Benjamin Benjamin," Mrs. Fowler shot back. "Now get in line."

Benny felt as if his head could explode. He wanted to kick her. He wanted to kick her in her bony shins *so bad.*

He kicked a big hole in the front of his own costume instead before taking his place at the back of the line, mumbling, "No, people just ***cheat*** in this school."

"Benjamin-Benjamin, Benjamin-Benjamin..." the kids chanted in a whisper as they plodded back to class.

Ann waited patiently with her bike outside Whitney Elementary. Other kids scampered by, eager to get home and prepare for more parties, pumpkin carving, and trick-or-treating.

Benny finally emerged dragging his costume behind him—the arm and leg tubes still stuffed inside it.

Ann noticed the big hole kicked through the front of it.

"Bad day, huh?" she asked.

Benny stayed mute as they hefted the costume onto Ann's bike rack and she walked the bike toward home with

Benny at her side.

"I was thinking... we should make Halloween cupcakes when we get home," Ann suggested, hoping to cheer him up. "Wanna help?"

Ann and Benny arrived home just as Randy and Tony did. They were pulling a wheelbarrow full of pumpkins of various odd sizes and shapes.

"Only a penny a pound at Miller's!" Randy explained. "And he gave us an extra discount for taking all the ugly ones."

The garage door was open. Frank stood at the tool bench working on his laser. He looked over and noticed Benny's costume as the rest of the kids entered.

"Whoa," Frank laughed," What happened? Another... short circuit?"

"You might say that," Ann added gently, trying to ease the moment.

"Benny, I told you that you should have let *me* do the wiring," Frank teased.

"Shut up!" Benny yelled back, "That's cheating!"

"That's how you get ahead in this world," Frank snickered.

Benny took a swing at him, but Frank planted a hand at the top of Benny's little head to keep his shorter arms from being able to make any serious contact.

Back at Jefferson High, Miss Espy stayed late in order to clean up her room after a particularly busy, party-filled day. She stacked the last easel in the corner of the room, swept the candy wrappers and other debris accumulated from her four classes' Halloween parties into a pile, and dustpanned them up, dumping them in her trash bin. Returning the broom and dustpan to the closet, she washed her hands at the sink, then crossed to her desk to finally put her feet up.

She snatched a chocolate kiss from her almost-empty basket of treats, unwrapped it, and popped it into her mouth, feeling it melt on her tongue.

The rest of the school had gone dead-quiet hours ago. The sun was low, ready to set, and her room had grown dim—almost creepy.

Oooooh! It's so Halloweenie, she noted to herself with a chuckle.

She wadded the foil wrapper from her chocolate kiss and tossed it at her trash bin. It missed.

"Shoot."

She hauled herself up to retrieve the wad and crossed to hold it directly over the trash bin, and dropped it in.

The wad went straight in but hit the side of a paper cup and bounced right back out and onto the floor again. She growled as it rolled under her desk just out of reach, making her have to go to her knees and dig for it.

While still seated on the floor, this time she carefully hand-placed the wad in the bin so it couldn't escape again.

It was only then she looked up and realized the one thing she forgot to do: erase the chalkboard.

"Shoot," she sighed again.

She grunted up to grab a long felt eraser bar from the tray at the base of the chalkboard and had a go at the perspective lesson she'd drawn there during her morning class.

As the eraser did its work, removing her drawing while accumulating dust as it went, she wiped it across a dark area of slate between her drawing's vanishing lines,

72

leaving some smudges that, at a glance, almost looked like a human *eye?*

Huh... she thought, and rubbed at it and around it a bit more with the chalky eraser.

Dust accumulated more heavily on it, revealing... it was definitely the image of an eye, with an ear, and the side of someone's head!

She got chills as she rubbed further—all alone in her now almost-dark, dead-quiet, *Halloweenie* classroom—rubbing higher, then lower, then higher again, revealing more and more of the mysterious image emerging there. It was large, forcing her to stand on tiptoe to reveal the top of it. When she was finally finished erasing the whole board she stepped back to get a full view.

The chalk dust revealed a faint, ghostly, eerie portrait of Bill Bobbs staring back at her with "Let Me Pass" scrawled in block letters beneath it.

Miss Espy felt her knees buckle.

From one end of the door-table Ann handed orange-frosted chocolate cupcakes to Benny while he used an icing bag to draw spiders on top of them with black frosting. At the other end of the table Randy and Tony scraped bowls of slop and seeds from the carcasses of their oddly shaped pumpkins.

Appropriately creepy music, *Chilling, Thrilling Sounds of the Haunted House*, played from the stereo.

Randy held up a lumpy pumpkin and turned it around for all to see. Ugly lumps scattered over the squash's skin resembled acne.

"I can't believe no one wanted this great pumpkin," he beamed.

He dug into the pumpkin and misshapen teeth appeared to fill a crooked mouth and then he fashioned wire braces for them. He paused again, then added a pair of their dad's old engineer's glasses at a cockeyed angle to create a kind of goofy, awkward-teenager jack-o-lantern.

"Lookie!" He commanded turning it around to show his siblings.

They all laughed in approval.

Randy crossed to the counter to start another, grabbing the biggest one next.

"Save the big one for Dad," Ann suggested.

Randy nodded in agreement and grabbed one that looked like a giant peanut instead, held it up and rotated it, contemplating its possibilities.

Back at the table, Tony announced, "Finished!" spinning his creation around for all to see. He had carved a pear-shaped gourd with tiny, close-set squinty eyes and a gaping mouth spewing some of the stringy, slimy pumpkin guts and seeds as barf.

Everyone laughed even harder than before, including Randy.

Randy sighed, "You win."

"I say we spoil our dinner," Ann proclaimed, winking at her brothers and unwrapping one of their finished cupcakes from a serving platter to take a bite. The others needed no persuading.

Tony and Randy reached for their treats with pumpkin slimed hands, dotted with seeds.

"No!" Ann shouted. "You'll yuck them all up. *Jeez—* wash your hands first!"

She pulled back the platter.

Her brothers scowled at her.

"You're not the boss of me!" Randy blurted, grabbing

a cupcake anyway.

"Yeah," added Tony, grabbing one for himself too. "You're not our..."

Frank burst in through the laundry room from the garage, eyes agog, and not because his siblings now all had black-lipped, icing-stained, zombie mouths.

"You are not going to believe *this*," he warned.

They heard the front door open followed by Matty's quick footfalls as he dashed into the kitchen to hide behind Ann.

"Cupcakes!" Frank grabbed one and stuffed it in his mouth, almost in a single bite.

"Matty...?" Ann asked in a whisper, "What's *wrong*, honey? Where's *Dad*?"

"Urr unna zee," Frank mumbled, his mouth filled with icing and cake.

Ed entered the kitchen with a voluptuous young platinum blond woman in a low cut, hot pink miniskirt.

A woman's shriek pierced out of the stereo followed by ominous low organs chords.

Tony's eyes went as wide as his icing-blackened grin.

Randy did a cartoon double-take.

Ann went into a frozen black-lipped gape.

Frank grabbed a second cupcake and inched back to observe the situation from a safer distance.

"These are my children," Ed said, smiling sweetly at the woman. He then turned to all of them with a hint of a scowl, and added, "Kids, this is Miss Sabrina Southern."

"Oh, Ed! They're all so adorable!" she gushed in a breathless Marilyn Monroe manner, making it almost feel like she was dressed for Halloween rather than actually like this in real life?

"The feeling is mutual," Tony grinned back, nudging

Randy.

"The fresh one there is Tony," Ed explained. "That's Randy, Benny, Frank, and my daughter, Ann," he continued.

Matty dashed for the sliding glass door to escape to the back yard, letting Chaos and several kittens in as he did.

"Matty there you already met," Dad added, pointing after him.

"Hello, poochie!" Sabrina cooed as Chaos licked at her hand with a slobbering tongue, then, in his excitement at her attention, peed at her feet.

"Oh!" she exclaimed, hopping back.

"Chaos, **bad boy!**" Ed snarled.

He grabbed Chaos by the collar and handed him to Randy with a gruff gesture.

"Take care of this," he ordered.

Randy dragged the hyperactive Chaos out to the back yard while Ed grabbed a big wad of paper towel to mop up the pee and a second wad for Sabrina's shoes.

"I'm *terribly* sorry," Ed sighed, shooting narrow-eyed glances at his kids.

Ann finally came out of her stupor just as the stereo emitted a roar of "thunder and rain."

She crossed to her dad and stepped on the paper towel he was wiping at the floor with, stopping him.

"Daddy, can I talk to you in *private* for a sec?"

"Not right now, sweetheart."

"Benny, finish this up for Dad, please?" Ann requested and turned her attention back to her father. "Dad, I need to talk to you. Family business!"

She gripped her father's arm, forcefully yanking him toward the hallway.

"Give me a sec, Sabrina," Ed apologized. "The boys

will entertain you."

He turned back to Ann, "Now, what's so *damned* important?"

"It's private," Ann retorted pulling him from the room.

Back in the kitchen, Sabrina proclaimed, "My, what amazing pumpkins!" while scanning their wacky array.

"I'll say," Randy replied, scanning Sabrina's ample cleavage and arching his eyebrows at Tony, who smirked back.

Matty quietly slipped in from the yard. He looked at Benny, who tossed the urine-soaked paper towels in the bin with an, "*Ulck!*"

Matty crossed to create his stairway out of drawers to reach the windowsill above the sink—and Lugee.

Benny joined him to cleanse his hands of dog pee.

"You okay?" Benny whispered to Matty.

"Yeah," Matty whispered, and worked his way back down.

Matty approached Sabrina, hands behind his back, wearing his most manipulatively angelic look and smiled adorably up at her.

"Hello, there," she giggled back," Not shy anymore?"

Matty shook his curly-haired head, still smiling sweetly. He brought an empty palm from behind his back, extended it to her, and coyly asked," Can I have a penny, please?"

"Why, sure cutie!" Sabrina responded, opening her purse to dig around in its bottom, emerging with a handful of loose coins. "Here you go, you can have *all* of these."

Matty examined them, slipped them into his pocket, and smiled up again.

"Would you like to meet Lugee?" he asked.

"Who's Lugee?"

The stereo hissed the sound effect of a lit fuse.

"My pet slug," Matty answered, bringing his other hand out from behind his back to shove Lugee right under Sabrina's nose.

It seemed to the other kids as if Matty had managed to turn Sabrina to stone.

Lugee oozed across Matty's extended palm, its upper tentacles slowly extending to expose tiny black beady eyes that stared and wobbled up at her.

Sabrina lifted her hands to cover her mouth as she started to gag.

"Down the hall and to the left," Frank pointed, as Sabrina dashed out.

The record hit the "explosion" effects, as if on cue.

"You're a wicked little bugger," Frank chuckled.

Matty extended his empty palm, making a "gimme" sign as Frank and Benny dug in their pockets to each drop a well-earned penny into it.

But not Randy.

"No way, Jose. You scared her off just when we were getting friendly."

"No dice," replied Tony too, slugging his baby brother in the arm instead of giving him a penny.

In the upstairs bathroom, Ed finished washing any dog pee off his hands while Ann scrubbed at her stained lips and gave him an earful.

"Daddy, you're not thinking clearly. How could you date that *awful* girl?!"

"Seems to me you're the one who's been pestering

me to date again."

"Date, not *adopt*! She's young enough to be your *daughter*!"

"She isn't bossy enough."

"You *need* my advice," Ann scolded, but it was clear she wasn't getting through to her father so she pulled rank on him adding, "What would *Momma* think?"

"*Enough*, Ann!" he snapped back, throwing the towel down on the counter and causing Ann to sit down on the edge of the tub, sensing she had gone a step too far.

"I loved your mother more than I've ever loved anyone else in the world. No one could ever take her place!"

He paced a bit, trying to calm down and, seeing the towel, folded and rehung it while he continued in a softer, more reflective tone.

"I'm... not looking for a replacement. I'm simply tired. Tired of being alone. Can you *understand* that?"

He turned to face Ann, who, rather than understanding, stared back defiantly, arms crossed. "I *wish* I was alone," she snipped back. "Oh, to have even a *moment* alone..."

"Well," he finished, rubbing the back of his neck, "It's different for me. You need to appreciate that."

"Daddy, if you go out with that girl, I'll *never* speak to you again."

"Suit yourself. You'd be doing me a favor. Of course, you never let me tell you *why* she's here," he dangled.

Ann looked up and cocked her head.

"I couldn't very well drive my new car *and* the station wagon, which will now become *your* car, home all by myself."

"My... *what?!*"

"If you're going to finish out the year at Jefferson

High after we move, you'll need to ***drive*** there, now, won't you...?"

"***My*** car?!"

Ann bolted from the room.

The thundering beat of Ann's footfalls on the stairs rousted the rest of the kids to join her in the driveway where a dinged-up, well used seafoam green 1962 Chevy Nova sat next to their family wagon.

Ed caught up with them as Ann and the rest of the kids circled the Nova.

"Oh, It's so *ugly*... but great!" Ann exclaimed.

She ran over to give a hug to the station wagon, then circled around both cars to give her dad a big hug too.

"And I won't have to change schools. Thank you," she sighed.

"I thought you weren't talking to me," Ed smirked.

"Oh, Daddy!"

"Now I won't have to switch schools either!" Frank realized. "I can ride in the wagon with Ann."

"And then have you drive there for another *two years*? Oh, no. *Just* Ann. And *only* because she's graduating this year," Ed declared.

"Naturally," Frank huffed, then added with a smirk, "Dad, you *did* know in Spanish 'Nova' means 'No Go,' right?"

A recomposed Sabrina came out to join them in the driveway.

Ann leaned over to kiss her Dad on the cheek and whisper, "I'm sorry I... jumped to conclusions."

"You didn't," he whispered back.

Ed took Sabrina's hand and escorted her to the passenger side of the Nova, then circled around to get in on the driver's side as the kids gathered. Ed started the car and rolled down his window to address them all.

"I'm taking Sabrina to dinner. You kids are on your own tonight. Ann's in charge. I won't be late so don't leave a mess."

Ed rolled up his window and turned to say something they couldn't hear to Sabrina, who giggled into her hand as they pulled out and took off down the road.

"But… it's *Halloween*…" Tony sighed.

Ann circled the station wagon again, beaming, contemplating the possibilities it would allow her.

"He didn't even carve his pumpkin," Benny groused.

"And we saved him the *big* one," Randy added.

"That's okay," Frank grinned, narrowing his eyes as the Nova rounded the corner, "I have a better plan for it."

It seemed like old times with all the neighborhood kids gathered around the Benjamin's front lawn once word got out.

Randy had moved the stereo speakers to blast their "scary sounds" record out the front windows.

The brick planter displayed a line-up of their weird and wonderful jack-o-lanterns, all eerily candle-lit for the evening.

Frank plopped the giant, uncarved pumpkin in the center of the lawn, lit a cherry bomb, and dropped it in a tidy hole he had drilled into the top of it.

"*FIRE IN THE HOLE!*" he hollered as he and all the kids ran for cover.

With an echoing boom, a sphere of pulverized pumpkin rind, guts, and seeds blasted all the way to the middle of the street as the hoard of costumed kids let out a roar of enthusiastic approval. It was a great way to start everyone's evening of trick-or-treating.

The Benjamins were at it again.

A chunk of pumpkin slime hit the Coe's kitchen window with a wet thud, startling Mrs. Coe.

Hearing the explosion outside made Ross, who was dressed as the Frankenstein monster, antsy.

"I hate Halloween," Mrs. Coe grumbled, struggling to tie the back of Ross's costume for him while he fidgeted anxiously.

"*Maaaaaaaamm...* hurry! I'm *missing* it all! An' all the good candy will be *gone!*"

"Hold still! There."

"Yaaaaaaaaaayyyy!!!" Ross squealed, running to get his pillowcase.

"Wait, Ross," She scolded, gripping him by a shoulder and yanking him back.

She took to a knee in front of him and stared directly into his face.

"No cupcakes! No homemade cookies! Only wrapped candy. You hear me? You don't realize how dirty other people are. And especially, no *apples*...."

"Oh, for the love of **God**, let the boy *alone*, Joy," Mr. Coe mumbled from behind his newspaper.

Tony, Benny, and Matty snaked their way through

the sidewalks teeming with kids in costumes. Tony figured this would be his last Halloween to trick-or-treat—next year he would be too old—so he decided to make this one count—he was a man on a mission. His two younger brothers could barely keep up.

They wore minimalist costumes: plain, dark clothing and pressed-plastic, pre-fab masks.

It was all part of Tony's optimization plan.

Quickly and systematically, they worked their way door by door, raising their masks to check the quality of each item proffered, until they reached the end of the block. The last door was where old Mr. and Mrs. White lived. They were nice—probably gave out the good stuff.

They pulled their masks back down and approached the open door with a loud, "Trick-r-treet!"

"Happy Halloween!" Mrs. White greeted with a sweet smile, dropping a treat into each of their bags.

"Thank you."

As they headed back to the sidewalk they lifted their masks and dug inside to find out what kind of tasty booty they got from the Whites.

"Raisins? *Ulck*," Benny gagged.

All three tossed their boxes on the Whites' lawn, already littered with many other little boxes of raisins.

Back at the Benjamin house a group of small kids rang the bell and yelled, "Trick-r-treeet!"

Randy answered the door, oozing catsup through his vampire teeth and holding a rat in each hand.

"Munch on **these!!!**" he cackled.

The kids screamed and turned away just as Frank

dropped a bloody hangman with a choking scream and a thud from above the porch roof to dangle overhead, causing them to scream even louder and run for their lives—several dropped their bags, spilling candy they didn't wait to retrieve, and some didn't even bother to retrieve their bags at all.

Randy collected the spoils and retreated back into the house to await their next victims.

Tony, Benny, and Matty had made quick work of close to a mile of homes, their bags growing heavy with loot. They returned to the sidewalk to check what they just got— full-sized Hershey bars!

They nodded to each other in agreement and each dug out different plastic mask from their bags, switched masks, and approached the same house for seconds.

As the evening wore down, Ross Coe's last stop was the Benjamin's house. He dragged his now-bulging pillowcase up the steps and rang the bell, hollering, "Trick-r-treat!"

This time Ann answered, holding a covered dish. She opened it for Ross to take one, revealing Randy's rats inside instead of candy.

Ross jumped back as Ann smiled and cackled, oozing catsup through vampire teeth.

Ross squeaked and turned to run as Frank dropped the hangman again with a choking scream, causing Ross to abandon his heavy pillowcase altogether and dash for his life.

Ann hefted the pillowcase and returned inside.

Tony, Benny, and Matty had packed three masks each—having a lot of older siblings meant a lot of leftover Halloween masks.

They switched masks and approached a house giving out full-sized 3 Musketeers bars for the third time. Because it was late and the crowds had thinned, the teenager at the door caught on to their scam, but only after he had already given each of them their third bars.

"Hey!" he scolded, as they ran for the sidewalk, laughing. "You're cheating, you know!"

Benny turned back and lifted his mask to smile at their prey.

"That's how you get ahead in this world," he shot back.

It was candy-sorting time in the Benjamin living room; with the three older ones around the coffee table and the three younger ones on the floor, each counting their evening's spoils.

Matty had the largest pile—by *far*. For some reason, maybe due to his being little and cute, he had managed to collect a lot of extra treats during their candy-gleaning.

Randy got up to retrieve the bowl of the Tootsie Pops by the door that their dad had bought for them to give out.

"*Heh.* I don't think we gave out a single one of these!" Randy bragged, with a chuckle. "How do you want to split them up?"

"We did all the work here," Frank argued, indicating Ann and Randy in the comment, "So *we* should get them."

"No way!" Benny complained.

"Forget it!" Matty agreed.

"Unfair!" Tony growled.

"We'll split them all *evenly*," Ann countered, trying to play peacemaker and giving Frank a pleading look, hoping he would back down rather than escalate.

Frank sighed, "Fine. But those guys are *sooo* greedy," then returned to counting and dividing out the spoils he, Ann, and Randy had accumulated from the kids they scared off.

"One for me; one for Ann; one Randy. One, two for me; two for Ann; two for Randy. One, two, three for me; three for..." adding with a nod at his younger brothers.

"Um, Frank... you're not fooling anyone," Ann smirked through narrowed eyes.

"What do you mean?"

"You're not counting fair."

"Oh, really? It was an honest mistake."

"Right. Fix it or else." Ann held out a fist.

"Oh no, I'm so scared."

Ann reconfigured her fist to make it more threatening by extending her middle knuckle.

"I'm still your big sister and I can still beat you up if I have to," she threatened. "Knuckle out!"

"*Okay*, okay, I was only kidding," Frank conceded.

Randy, distributing the Tootsie Pops, ended with Matty, who was seated in the center of the floor.

"Put them *there*, please," Matty commanded, pointing to a pile of various types of pops and suckers.

Matty had organized his candies into neat, separate piles: Hershey's kisses, Tootsie Rolls, SweeTARTS, Pixy Stix, Necco Wafers, candy bars—which then all had sub-groups, some even by color.

Randy examined it all. He silently signaled the others, who then looked over to see what he saw.

More non-verbal looks and nods of agreement, whispers, and devious grins exchanged between everyone but Matty, who hummed the tune of *Monster Mash* to himself as he continued sorting and counting.

Once Frank finished the dole-out, Ann dumped her night's take into a paper bag and got up.

"I'm gonna have another cupcake," she announced, and headed out of the room.

Benny stuffed his candy back into his bag and followed Ann out with a, "Me too."

Frank pushed his haul off of the coffee table and into a bag, and got up.

"I better go blow out the pumpkins."

"I'll help," Randy added, exiting the front door with him.

Only Matty and Tony were left.

Tony tipped his bag on its side and quickly plowed his candy piles from the floor into it, stood, and taking a little too long to come up with an excuse to leave, finally shrugged and said, "I need to go to the bathroom."

It didn't really matter what he said. Matty wasn't listening. He was still sorting Mars, Baby Ruth, Pay-Day, Butterfingers, and 3 Musketeers bars. He finally looked up.

Huh.

He was all alone.

And the house had gone... completely dead quiet.

With a *ka-chunk*, the power went off, plunging the

house into total darkness.

"*Hey!*" Matty yelled.

A scuffling commotion followed, full of muffled giggles, Matty's grunts, and scrambling feet before the lights came up with another *ka-chunk* to reveal Matty, still sitting alone in the center of the room, wailing, now buried in a pile of his thoroughly re-mixed-up candy.

Chapter Five

House VS Home

Ed's alarm clock rang. His feet hit the cold floor a little more slowly than usual, but he set off on his morning ritual anyway: rap, bang, yell; bang, rap, yell.

When he was almost back to his room Randy popped out of his bedroom door holding a half-eaten 3 Musketeers candy bar.

"Daaaaad! It's **Saturday!**"

Ed turned back as Randy whipped his candy bar around to hide it behind his back.

Ed saw it but, picking his battles, pretended not to.

"Do you kids want to find a new house or *not*?"

By the time Ed got Chaos and the last of the kittens removed to the back yard, gathered up the paperwork Sabrina had given him, locked the house, and made it to the station wagon, the kids were all loaded and patiently waiting for him.

Ann sat behind the wheel.

"Right," Ed sighed, rolling his eyes.

He opened the driver's side door and snapped, "Over, A. J. Foyt," motioning her to slide over to the passenger's side front seat, then got in.

"I have my permit," she pouted, fiddling with the radio tuner. "How am I gonna *learn* to drive if you don't ever *let* me drive?"

She stopped the knob on the Beatles', "Hard Day's Night."

Ed snapped the radio off.

"If you are going to drive *this* car then you first need to know *how*. Every car is a little different. Pay attention and watch everything I do *as I do it*—I'll explain what I'm doing as I go."

All the boys unfastened their seatbelts to lean over the seat and watch their dad explain.

"Back in your belts, boys, I'm not gonna tell you again!" Ed scolded.

They all obeyed but not without a chorus of huffing, sighing, and moaning.

Ed handed Frank a map along with the first sheet of paper in his folder.

"Frank, you're navigator. Find this address and let me know when you're set to give directions. Now, Annie, pay close attention."

Ed slowly and meticulously started the car and backed out of the driveway narrating all the way while Frank hollered directions, Benny and Tony quit watching and got into a slap fight, Randy slipped a Tootsie Roll into his mouth while no one was looking, and Matty smushed his nose against the window and *arf*ed, pretending to be a dog.

After a wrong turn and a bit of backtracking, the Benjamins pulled up to a Tudor-style home, with a faux-beams and stucco exterior, a mini-tower over the entrance, and a crenelated chimney.

Sabrina waited in the shade of the inset entrance, waving to them.

Ann moaned.

"I don't care to see this house *or Sabrina*, and I don't want to move! Therefore, I refuse to participate. This is a sit-in," she announced to her dad, crossing her legs to sit Indian-style.

She glanced at her brothers, hoping for some sibling solidarity.

Her brothers were halfway out of the car already, charging en masse toward the entrance and leaving Ann to stage a sit-in of one.

Ed laughed, "Suit yourself."

Like cockroaches, the brothers spread throughout the home's interior, searching behind every door, in every closet, and around every corner. In the dining room, Ed and Sabrina found Matty at a tall window.

"Lugee could live here, I guess," he concluded. "Lots of light."

Sabrina cringed.

The distant thunder of charging sneaker-clad feet drew Ed toward a rear wing of the house off the family room, an obvious and architecturally incongruous additional row of bedrooms.

Tony had already staked his claim, "My room!"

"Not fair, that's the biggest one," complained Randy.

Ed scanned past the brothers. He frowned, "There's no bathroom down here?" he questioned Sabrina.

"No, she replied, "but the previous owners did just redecorate the two baths upstairs," she added in the relentlessly positive manner of all real estate agents.

"Hmm," Ed responded, setting his jaw. "Not even a powder room on this level?"

"You know, I can tell this place just isn't for you," Sabrina relented, "but I have better ones to show you."

"I hope so," Ed replied, giving her a side glance and

reappraisal. "Okay. Let's move on."

They returned to the station wagon to find Ann belted into the driver's seat.

Ed opened the door.

"Don't test me, Annie."

He popped her seatbelt latch, and motioned her over so he could follow Sabrina to the next stop where Ann continued her pouty, one-person sit-in.

This second house was on a large lot and was huge. Once a grand shingle-style Victorian, it was now definitely a major fixer-upper. Both the house and yard showed pretty heavy signs of neglect, with dangling shingles and dry rot visible on the wide wrap-around porch.

The boys immediately took to the back yard, and it was no wonder. It was as densely overgrown as Tarzan's jungle, with giant Bird of Paradise trees and beautiful mature sycamore and oak trees shading it. One of the larger oaks held the remains of a treehouse. There were the cracked and dry remains of a large koi pond with a bridge and a rotten trellis only held up by a network of old, ropy grape vines.

With seven bedrooms and four baths, plus a large playroom down in the basement, it certainly more than suited their practical needs. And it was just the kind of unusual house Ellen would have been eager to revive.

If she had been there with him, Ed would have jumped on it despite its condition.

He turned the spigot on in the kitchen sink. Rusty water sputtered out before eventually clearing. A distant pipe somewhere in the cellar moaned in protest.

"It *is* at the bottom end of your price range," Sabrina said, apologetically.

Price wasn't the issue for Ed on this one. He actually

liked the house; it made him think of Ellen. But her not being there with him, elbows-deep in it, and him not having her there to slather all her magic touches of life back into the old place only made the house seem... he didn't want to think about it. Too much pain.

It was time to clear the slate, he told himself. Put the past away.

"Let's move on."

Ann had belted herself into the driver's seat again, this time gripping tight to the wheel when she saw them coming.

Ed rolled his eyes, opened the door, snapped open the latch on her belt, and physically pulled her out. She stomped around to the passenger side again, climbed in, and slammed the door.

They did a quick stop at the Red Barn for some burgers, fries, and sodas to eat in the car on the way to meeting Sabrina at the third house.

This house was every bit as overly-manicured as the last one was shabby. An equally overly-manicured realtor stood guard at the door.

"Wait!" he insisted, trying to hold back the tsunami of Benjamin boys barreling past him.

He turned to Ed and Sabrina.

"*Please* control these children!" he pleaded. "This is a model residence."

"Right, I'll get right on that," replied Ed, with a laugh.

Inside, it was all picture windows, blonde furniture, and cream wall-to-wall carpeting. Fresh flowers were arranged in each room. And in the kitchen, the Benjamin boys had discovered—and were cleaning out—a platter of freshly baked cookies.

The fussy realtor rushed in, "No, no. Those aren't for eating. They're ambiance!"

"Sorry," Ed apologized. "Kids are kids—cookies are cookies." He turned to his brood, "Boys—leave the ambiance alone! Outside!"

Then to Sabrina, *"Ambiance...?"*

She shrugged back, "It's a realtor thing. The smell sells."

She guided Ed out of the room, leaving the realtor to rearrange his half-demolished cookie platter back into something more presentable while evil-eyeing the boys in the back yard.

It was certainly a pristine, well-appointed home, Ed thought—five bedrooms, three full baths. It was perfect.

Maybe a little too perfect?

The back yard had a wide covered veranda and sparkling pool. Sabrina escorted him out in time for him to prevent Randy from pushing Tony into it. From behind, he heard a squeaking noise and turned to see the other scowling agent cleaning his kids' fresh hand-prints off of the sliding glass door.

"It's a bit too, well, *fussy* for us," Ed suggested. "But it does have everything we need, and the area is good. What are they asking for it?"

The boys heard their dad roar with laughter and then motion to them that it was time to go.

This time, Ann sat waiting—in the passenger seat.

Ed relented. He walked around the car to open her passenger door and urge her out.

"Really?" Ann squeaked.

Ed nodded.

She dashed under his arm and out past him as he climbed in, mentally preparing himself for what was to follow.

Ann got into the driver's seat and closed the door.

"Woman driver alert! Woman driver alert!" whooped Frank as he popped open his door and scrambled out.

"Our turn to protest!" added Tony, scrambling for the open door, followed by Benny.

"*Mayday*! Bail out! Bail out!" Randy mocked, ejecting himself from the other side to roll across the sidewalk melodramatically.

Only Matty remained in the back of the station wagon. He looked at Ann, then at his brothers and sat pat— but fastened and tightened his seatbelt.

"Okay, Annie," began Ed, loud enough to be heard by the boys at the curb. "Check that the transmission is in park, then turn the key and start the car."

Ann followed his instructions and the wagon roared into life with her foot heavy on the accelerator.

"Easy on the gas!" shouted her father.

"Fine!" she snapped back.

The boys, leapt back from car.

Ann raised her foot and the car settled into idle.

"Right. Now put your foot on the brake and move the transmission into D for drive. Now *slowly* ease up on the brake..."

The car began to slowly roll forward.

Randy turned to his brothers.

"He isn't really going to ditch us, *is he?*"

They all looked at the car slowly accelerating away, looked at each other, then back at the car.

"Dad...?"

Inside the car, Ed continued, "Now check your rear view and side mirrors for oncoming traffic."

"It's clear, Daddy," Ann replied.

"Good. Now look back over your shoulder to be sure, then take your foot completely off the brake and just lightly push the accelerator when it's clear, while pulling further away from the curb."

Ed turned his head to assure himself there were no approaching cars.

The car started to roll forward in earnest as Ann barely touched the gas pedal.

The boys lit into a jog to keep up and continued shouting, "Dad? Wait! *Wait!* We're sorry! Don't go. Dad!"

"A *little* more gas, Annie," Ed coached, smiling.

Screech—rear wheels spun, smoke rose as her foot hit the pedal too hard!

The boys leapt back from the curb.

"Let up!" shouted Ed. "Brake!"

"Yelling doesn't help!"

Screech, forward, *brake*, jerk, *screech*, the station wagon fitfully started working its way more quickly down the street.

"It's like Disneyland!" Matty chirped with delight.

"They're getting away!" Randy gasped, pushing Tony forward.

"After them!" Frank yelled, taking off in a full run to follow the accelerating wagon while Benny struggled to keep up with all his older brothers.

Toward the end of the block, Ed told Ann, "Okay, pull over here and wait."

Ann nudged the steering wheel over a bit too tightly

and aimed the car toward the curb and a stop. Ed grabbed the wheel and corrected the turn before she hit the curb, "Easy, Annie. Smooth moves are the key."

And Ann brought the car to a halt.

"That was fun," shouted Matty from the rear seat, "Do it again!"

After a good scolding and the order, "No speaking when Ann is driving," Ed managed to get Ann to white-knuckle them to their next stop without much further drama and fewer jerky stops and rear wheel-screechings. Mr. Plummer had taught her well and she checked her mirrors regularly and got all her signals right.

Ed noted, with a private smile, that he didn't need to remind the boys to fasten their seat belts this time.

Ann scraped the curb when she pulled up to the fourth house.

Through the car windows they saw a cute but *very* small one-story Dick and Jane style home, almost like a playhouse that had barely grown up to become real.

"Nope," Ed wheezed. "Put her in park and wait here," he instructed Ann, as he jumped out to have a quick chat with Sabrina about skipping this one and moving on.

Overcorrecting this time, Ann parked a full three feet from the curb in front of the next house just as a realtor was adding a "SOLD!" sign over the "For Sale" placard in front.

Sabrina waved an arm out of her car window for them to continue to follow and they were off again.

There was only one open parking spot when Ann pulled the station wagon up in front of a clean, simple, large, two-story contemporary house.

Ed sighed. "That's okay, honey. Just pull into the driveway."

"It's not a problem, Daddy. We already practiced parallel parking in Driver's Ed."

Ann pulled the wagon forward, next to Sabrina's car. She shifted into reverse, twisted around to watch as she backed up, did a 45° reverse, slipped in and straightened out the car in one simple swift maneuver.

"Whoa!" gasped Frank.

"Very nice, Ann," complimented Ed, with an edge of surprise in his voice.

Sabrina chatted with the house's representing agent in the middle of the broad green front lawn as the tide of Benjamin boys erupted from the car and swept past them, headed for the house.

Back in the car, Ed turned to Ann.

"I gave a little, now *you* give a little," he suggested. "Come on, Annie. Look at this one with the rest of us."

She knit her brow, glanced soulfully at him, and then managed a wan smile.

"I know you don't want to," Ed sighed, "But please. *For me*. We all have to move on."

"As long as that's what we are doing," she relented, unfastening her belt. "Moving on, not... giving up."

A large open-beam living room adjacent to an airy, skylit entryway fronting a stairway created an outdoors-brought-inside feeling to the house. As Ed and Ann entered, Randy met them by sliding down the bannister and landing with a flourish, flashing an "okay" sign of approval.

"Lay off the acrobatics, Randy. This isn't a jungle gym," scolded Ed.

He turned to his daughter, "Give the place a chance, Annie. Check it out before you check it off."

Ann took a desultory look at the kitchen, which *was* nicer *and* prettier than theirs. She decided to mope off back towards the car before anything else won a comparison contest when she noticed there was a mother-in-law suite just off the entry downstairs.

Her curiosity got the better of her and she took a peek.

It was large, with a comfy-looking built in window seat beneath a bay window. It was isolated from the main house, and had its own en suite bathroom.

It was hard not to be completely charmed into picturing it as her own private world.

Frank, Randy, and Tony stood in the middle of the large, open back lawn discussing the possibilities of building a tree fort in a large oak tree in the back corner of the yard while Benny practiced cartwheels across the soft grass.

Matty knelt next to a flowerbed and lifted the broad leaves of a hosta to happily discover several slugs and some friendly earwigs hiding there.

Ed found a large upstairs bathroom with two sinks, walk-in shower, and a full tub. He tried the faucet. The water was clean with good pressure. His eye caught the boys already playing together on the back lawn out of the bathroom window.

When Ann exited the mother-in-law suite, she noticed her dad seated at the dining room table in discussions with Sabrina and the other realtor. She spied from around the corner. She couldn't catch all the words but was able to intuit that her father had asked for the price. After a moment of hesitant disbelief, and raising a hand to his ear like he hadn't heard right, the agent repeated herself. Her dad smiled and they shook hands.

Ann retreated to wait in the passenger seat of the station wagon.

She was torn. Her brothers, like stray pets, were willing to make any place with food and a bed to sleep in their home. And the mother-in-law suite was a nice space to claim as her own, the kind of room that she had dreamed of forever. Was she merely being stubborn? Was moving there such a bad thing? But it meant that the home they had all grown up in, the one she thought of as Momma's house, was soon to be a thing of the past.

And she started to cry.

Ed had made an offer on the house that very day, but there was a hold up in the sale—something about having to wait for the current owners to find and purchase another house to move into first? The Benjamin kids didn't really pay all that much attention to what their dad related to them about it, they only absorbed the part about the possibility of their move being delayed at least a month or two—until after the holidays.

Ann took this as a good omen—fate didn't want her family to move, she decided. She still had time to show her father how wrong he was, how their home, *this* home, her *mother's* home, was the *family's* home.

She didn't yet know how to do it, but she was determined to find a way.

Chapter Six

Missing Pieces

The Great Pumpkin Explosion, as it came to be known in the neighborhood, re-established the Benjamin house as the focal point for the kids on their block. In spite of their parents' disapproval—or maybe because of it—more of them began hanging out there again. After all, there wasn't any supervision at the Benjamin house; you could eat all the snacks you wanted there; you didn't have to worry about putting your feet on the furniture; you could belch without having to say, "Excuse me,"—it was cool.

They had to be stealthier, and some would lie about where they had been when asked, but there was never a dull moment for anyone brave enough to drop by the Benjamins.

On this particular day, the event of interest concerned Benny blasting off a new water rocket he had received for his birthday.

"...forty-nine, fifty," Benny counted as he pumped far more pressurized air into it than the instructions suggested, making the base of the rocket hiss ominously. "Stand back."

Randy, Tony, and Matty along with several neighbor kids all backed away a bit as Benny prepared the launch, judging the wind direction with a spit-wetted finger and aiming its trajectory accordingly.

Matty settled himself on the raised bed along the front of the patio near the wooden fence separating their house from the Coes' to observe. He heard a scuffling sound on the other side of the fence and glanced over to see an eye peering through a knothole.

Ross was spying on them.

Benny released the catch, letting the rocket blast skyward with a sharp sputter of moisture and air.

The rocket shot almost straight up in an elegant, tight helix to spontaneous sounds of awe. It arced at the top and sailed nose down to land with a soft thud only a few feet from where Benny stood—the group applauded the picture-perfect launch and recovery, and Tony and Matty patted Benny on the back for his stunning success.

"Big deal," Randy scoffed. "I can make it go higher than that without even pumping it."

"No you *can't*," Tony countered.

"Put your *money* where your *mouth* is," Benny challenged.

"Okay," Randy grinned. "A *quarter*."

The group gasped and glanced about silently. Things had just gotten serious. A whole *quarter*? Real money was on the line.

"Any takers?" Randy offered, raising his quarter in the air and wiggling it as an enticement. "Or... are you all *chicken*?"

Since it was Benny's rocket *and* he wasn't going to let anyone call him chicken, he dug a quarter out of his pocket and held it up. Slowly a few other kids followed.

Tony hesitated.

"Well," Randy mocked, smirking at Tony. "Mister all talk and no action."

Tony was known for being tight with his money. When all the other kids were broke, Tony always seemed to still have a few bucks in what the others called his "magic wallet." But now he was surrounded by his brothers and the local kids, being called "chicken" and "all talk."

Randy knew he had him on the hook even before Tony reluctantly held up his coin.

102

All bets noted, Randy pointed to Benny's rocket.

"I'll need that—thank you," he requested, and Benny handed him the rocket and launcher.

Randy confidently strode toward the house and the others followed after him like a brood of baby ducklings. He headed to the kitchen and set both rocket and launcher on the counter next to the sink. He extracted a sheet of paper from the drawer next to the phone, folded it in half and unfolded it again to lay the creased paper flat on the counter.

Randy crossed to the pantry cupboard and retrieved the box of baking soda and the vinegar bottle.

As he did so, Tony slapped a palm to his own forehead, immediately realizing what Randy was up to.

Randy measured out two teaspoons of baking soda onto the creased paper and used the crease to carefully funnel the powder into the small opening at the end of the rocket. He held the rocket nose down over the sink and poured a thin stream of vinegar into the rocket too, quickly sealing it with the launcher and clipping it in place.

"GANGWAY!!!" he shouted while dashing for the front door as pressurized foam already began leaking from the base of the rocket.

"TEN... NINE... EIGHT," he counted down as he dashed outside. "SEVEN-SIX-FIVE-FOUR-THREE-TWO-**ONE**..." he blurted as fast as he could as the rocket hissed and spit.

He hit the middle of the front lawn followed by the gaggle of captivated kids, knelt, and shouted, "...***BLAST OFF!!!***"

Contrails of sour fizz shot from the rocket's base as it bolted skyward, higher and higher until it nearly vanished against the sun.

The crowd of kids went wild with cheers.

Benny started to worry it might never come back

down.

"Pay up, guys," Randy demanded, holding out a greedy palm followed by the reluctant clink of coins into it.

Matty glanced over at the knot hole in the fence.

Ross's eye was still there watching.

Benny's rocket was quickly visible again as its spent fuel gave way to gravity and it plummeted back to earth, gaining speed as it did.

"Run for cover!" Matty yelled as all the kids, save Benny, scattered so they wouldn't get beaned.

"Oh, NO!" shouted Benny.

Randy's hurried aim coupled with a light breeze had caused the rocket to veer off course and head for the Coe's front yard where it landed somewhere behind the separating fence.

Ross's eye left the knothole.

Great, thought Benny.

Randy sidled up to him, hand out to rub salt in the wound, "Pay up, Benny."

"Get my rocket back first," he countered.

"*You* get it!" Randy shot back, shoving him. "It's *your* rocket."

"That's not *fair*. You launched it—*you* go get it back. Otherwise, I'm not paying!"

Benny and Randy tussled and fists flew. Benny got a few impressive punches in, but Randy finally sat on him, dug a quarter out of his little brother's pocket, and let him go.

Randy strolled back to the house counting his cash, followed by Tony.

"I'll get it for you," Matty offered.

"No," Benny replied, "*I'll* get it—you stay in the yard."

Then Benny, followed by the neighborhood kids, marched over to the Coe's front yard, where Ross stood, one fat foot resting on top of Benny's rocket.

Benny steeled himself and approached Ross while the rest of the kids stayed safely on the sidewalk.

"You're standing on my rocket," Benny stated.

"It's in my yard, it's my rocket now."

"Give it back."

"Make me," Ross challenged, with a smug, bully's grin, stepping forward to shove Benny hard in the chest and knock him down.

Ross gloated in his advantage. He was well over a head taller and much larger than Benny.

What he and the rest of the kids on the sidewalk didn't realize was Benny was not the least bit intimidated by Ross Coe's size. Benny had to hold his own with three older brothers—Ross was no match for a kid who regularly battled giants. And Benny had just lost a fight with Randy, so he was hungry for a victory in battle.

Benny stood.

"Hand it over," he insisted as he moved closer to Ross, his fingers beginning to roll up into tight fists.

"Who's gonna make me?" Ross replied, showing his fists.

"Last chance," Benny warned.

Ross mocked him, pointing a finger to his own chin as if to say, "Go ahead and hit me."

Without hesitation and using his full body weight, Benny wound up and jab-punched Ross square in the face with the flat knuckles of his well-curled fist, knocking the bigger boy down with one, jaw-jarring, sound-barrier-cracking punch. The force of his punch set Ross flat on his back with his heels to the sky, like something out of a Daffy Duck cartoon.

The neighborhood kids gasped in surprise—then burst out laughing.

Ross squealed out in startled pain. He teetered up to an elbow and felt his lip. When he took away his hand there was blood on his fingers.

"Ross-Coe, Bosco! Ross-Coe, Bosco!" the kids all chanted, taunting him.

Benny snatched up his rocket and turned to see the crowd of chanting kids, who first looked with delight at the bleeding, mewling Ross, and then back at Benny with fresh admiration and awe.

Ross touched his sore mouth, yelped again, burst into tears, and ran for the house screaming, "*Maaaaaaaaaammm!!!*"

The neighborhood kids and Benny instantly shot off in all directions before Mrs. Coe could identify any of them.

Dinner was unusually calm and quiet, and the kids didn't know what to make of their dad. Even after it was explained to him what had occurred between Benny and Ross Coe that afternoon, he didn't really react the way he normally would, the way they all expected him to.

"We'll deal with it later," was his mantra for everything that evening.

Benny wasn't scolded for fighting. Instead, his father asked, "Did you win?"

"Yessir," replied Benny.

"Good. As long as you didn't start it and you didn't cheat."

Ann and Frank were shocked they weren't being blamed for not supervising their younger siblings and preventing the fight. Their father didn't even crab at them about their unfinished chores or the messy house.

He didn't seem to mind when Benny slipped away from the table early without permission to hold vigil at the front window, and... it all was just too *weird*.

"Did you have a good day at work?" Ann asked, trying to figure out if her dad was in a really good mood for some reason?

"The usual," was his reply, then he changed the subject, finally giving a clue as to what was distracting him. "I've got some... business to deal with tonight and I'll be out for a while. I want to find the dishes done, the lunches made, and everything spic and span when I get back."

"It would help if we had a housekeeper, Daddy," Ann countered, hoping his placid mood might make him more persuadable than usual.

"Ann—*no*," he answered curtly, "We've been over this. You kids need to learn to be responsible for yourselves. None of you finished any of your chores today—*yes*, I *noticed*. You guys better do them and clean this place up tomorrow, or there'll be hell to pay."

He stood and started to leave the room. "Your mother isn't here to do it for you anymore—so now you have to do it for yourselves."

Ann followed him, "But, Dad..."

Ed stood by the mirror in the entryway re-tidying his hair, re-checking his tie, and continuing the argument with Ann.

"No, no, no, no, **no!**" Ed repeat-fired back to Ann, just to make sure she knew where he stood, and that it really wasn't an argument, but a decision.

"But, Dad," Ann argued back, "What about *my* life? There's no way I can keep my grades up and make dinner every night and do all the crap you want me to do around here! We need to hire someone!"

107

He turned to face her, "I just bought a second car to help you, so don't you *dare* say I'm not supporting you. This whining is the thanks I get?! With all you kids to do chores around here it should be *easy* to get them done. There's no way I'm paying for a housekeeper and that's final!"

He opened the coat closet to get his coat. A Wiffle ball, a Hula Hoop, and several wire hangers spilled out.

"If you kids would just work together..."

"You don't *want* me to go to college!" Ann sobbed.

Tony wandered in carrying a cardboard box with Mommacat and a fresh litter of kittens inside.

"Wow, she had *eight* this time," he announced. "Dad, does the number of kittens have anything to do with the number of times...?"

Benny yanked the drapery chord, snapping the drapes shut and interrupted with an ominous, "They're coming!"

"Who's coming?" Ed asked as he rehung the escapee coat hangers and managed to hold the Hula hoop and kick the Wiffle ball back into the closet and closed the door on them, trapping them back inside, before the doorbell rang.

"The Coes," replied Benny.

Ed glanced at his watch and sighed in frustration.

Benny looked contritely at his dad, who motioned him over to come and stand next to him.

Ed opened the door revealing Mr. and Mrs. Coe with Ross at their side.

"Hello, we've been expecting you—won't you come in?" Ed offered.

"We'd rather not," Mrs. Coe clipped back.

Ed exhaled, and cut to the chase.

"Look, I'm just on my way out but Benny and the other kids told me what happened."

"Oh?" Mrs. Coe immediately countered, "Did they tell you that your boy hit my boy in the face with a **rock?!**"

Benny's eyes popped wide.

Ed looked at Benny; Benny shook his head vigorously.

This new twist interested the other Benjamin kids, who slowly gathered at the doorway with them.

"He said your son stole his rocket and refused to give it back without a fight, so he punched your son with his fist," Ed responded.

"He's lying!" Mrs. Coe snapped back. "He beat him with a rock! Ross said so. He could have *killed* my boy!"

It was obvious to the Benjamin kids that Ross must have concocted this story to hide his embarrassment over the fact that little Benny had knocked his block off.

"Benny doesn't lie!" Ann shot back.

Ed held Ann back and took a step closer to the Coe's.

"Look, your son is quite a bit bigger than my Benny. The kids tell me he's a bully and likes to pick on all the smaller kids," Ed countered, adding, "I think your boy just underestimated mine. Benny's used to fighting with his older brothers, so he's not afraid of your son."

Mrs. Coe turned to her husband.

"Ron...?"

Ron, who looked like he would have been happier to ignore the whole thing and be home reading the sports page, set his jaw and, reaching over, pulled Ross up by the collar to present to Ed.

Ross's split lip was the color of a ripe plum and twice its normal size.

Frank, Randy, and Tony all patted Benny on the back with pride.

"Really, Mr. Benjamin," Mr. Coe argued, "A fist couldn't do this much damage."

"Yes it could," Ed replied.

"You weren't *there!*" Mrs. Coe snapped back, "How would *you* know!"

"Because I taught all my kids how to fight back if they need to," Ed answered curtly while leaning in, causing the three Coes to step back. "Even Ann."

Mrs. Coe huffed, yanking Ross back so gruffly he let out a yelp.

"Well, obviously the neighborhood isn't safe around you Benjamins! If anything like this ever happens again, we'll call the *authorities!*"

"It won't," Ed answered, with narrowed eyes and clenched teeth. "Good evening."

He closed the door on the Coes and spun to face his stunned kids.

"Benny, *never*, under *any circumstances* are you to *ever* go near the Coe's *ever* **ever** again—do I make myself clear?!" he scolded.

Benny nodded.

"You're grounded for a week," Ed added.

"It wasn't *his* fault," Randy defended, "It was Bosco's!"

"Randy, **enough!**" Ed snapped back. "Case closed!"

He glared at his watch.

"And now I'm late and you guys have dishes to clean up..." he growled impatiently, pointing toward the kitchen, then turned to his daughter, "Right, Ann?"

Before she could answer, Frank jumped in, "You going out with Sabrina tonight?"

"Who...?"

Ed had to think for a moment, then remembered Sabrina and chuckled, shaking his head.

"No, no... I'm just going to a meeting." Ed pointed to Benny and Matty, adding, "You two—in bed by *nine*. Ann's in charge."

"But I need to go to the library tonight!" she whined.

"Ann—will you *please* be responsible for once?!" Ed snarled back as he bolted out the door in a trot.

"Practice what you preach," she grumbled back.

The kitchen clock read 10:30.

Although well past *all* their bedtimes, the Benjamin kids sat around the kitchen table eating ice cream sundaes while playing a cut-throat game of Hearts.

Ann wasn't officially playing, but was teaching Matty the game instead.

It was Matty's turn.

Ann examined the center pile, then scanned Matty's hand, and finally pointed to a card.

"*That* one."

Matty put down the three of hearts and Frank took the trick.

"Good, see? You made Frank take your heart. Now keep a watch on your high cards," Ann continued in a whisper.

Frank next led with the ace of hearts.

"Uh-oh," Ann whispered.

"What," Matty whispered back.

"It looks like Frank's trying to shoot the moon."

"Ann, can we cut the running commentary," Frank groused, annoyed at his sly intentions being broadcast aloud.

Both Benny and Tony glanced at Frank and re-sorted their cards while Randy examined his own hand, shrugged, and smiled.

"What's *shoot the moon*?" Matty asked in an even softer whisper.

"If you get all the hearts and the queen of spades you win the round and everyone else gets twenty-six points," Ann explained.

Frank led another high heart, collecting up more of them.

"Let's see..." Ann whispered, "You should try to stop him. Use one of your high cards to win a trick with a heart in it if you can."

"Ann, it's Matty's hand—let *him* play it!" Frank snapped.

"Getting nervous, are we?" Randy interjected with a smirk.

"You wish," Frank smirked right back, then led with the king of diamonds.

Randy, having no diamonds left, threw in a nine of hearts, but then, rethinking, took it back.

Frank slugged him.

"Put it back—you already played it."

Randy smiled and gently placed the card back in the pile, responding, "It's only a game."

Matty looked helpless and confused so he played a three of diamonds.

It was Benny's play next. He stared hard at his hand. He glanced nervously at Frank, then back at his hand, finally making a decision.

Benny played the ace of diamonds and took the hand—undoing Frank.

"Yay—way to go, Benny!" Ann cheered.

"Dammit, dammit, ***dammit...!***" Frank ranted as he leapt up, kicked over his chair, and threw his remaining cards across the room.

Benny ducked under the table as Frank, continuing his angry rant, slammed a hand against the edge of the table and sending the last melting scoop of Matty's sundae sliding onto the floor.

"Nice move, Frank! You're a great example to the little ones!" Ann scolded, then turning to Matty said, "Get a sponge, honey."

"***Shut up***, Ann!" Frank snapped back, "You're not **Mom** so stop trying to ***act like her!***"

The room went dead silent.

Everyone froze, wondering what would happen next, with Frank glaring at Ann and Ann staring back at him in anguish, tears welling in her eyes.

She dashed from the room.

Everyone else looked at Frank, who already regretted his outburst but was trying hard to cover with more bluster.

"Matty, get the damned sponge!" he snapped.

Matty scrambled to the sink while Benny climbed out from under the table. He and Tony collected cards off the floor together and Benny quietly counted the deck to make sure they had all the cards.

He set them on the table, then looked up at Frank.

"Sorry..." Benny apologized.

Frank shook his head at himself, finally coming out of his rage and reached over.

Benny flinched, but Frank patted him on the shoulder.

"It's not your fault, Benny. You played good. You did *exactly* what I woulda done," he admitted with a resigned sigh.

Frank looked around the room, then at his brothers.

"I'll clean up, you guys get to bed," Frank ordered.

"Yes... **Dad**," Randy mocked back and dashed from the room before Frank could slug him again, with Tony, Benny, and Matty close on his heels.

Frank rinsed the last bowl and placed it in the dishrack. He threw a dishtowel over his shoulder, rinsed the sponge, and crossed to wipe down and dry off the table. He got out a stack of lunch bags.

He glanced over to see Chaos looking in through the sliding glass door, wagging his tail, proudly sitting next to a fresh mound of his own poop.

Frank glanced over and noticed the Coes' lights were still on.

He tossed the sponge back into the sink, dried his hands, racked the towel, and lofted a lunch bag.

The Coe's doorbell rang several times. Mrs. Coe marched out of the bedroom wrapping her curlers in a floral silk scarf, and mumbled, "Who could *that* be at *this* time of night?"

She looked at her husband who was lost in the climax of his *Mannix* episode, and sighed.

"Oh, no really... don't get up, Henry—*I'll* get it!" she groused.

She opened the door to discover a brown paper lunch sack ablaze on her porch and instinctually lifted a foot to stomp it out, but stopped herself. She glanced at the

Benjamin house, retreated, and returned with a bucket of water instead.

Ed quietly entered the dark house. He glanced at the radium dial of his watch—it was 12:30.

He noticed the desk light had been left on in the kitchen.

Ed entered the dimly-lit kitchen, clicked on the overhead lighting, pulled a card out of his shirt pocket, and set on the counter by the phone before noticing Ann had been sitting alone at the table in the semi-darkness with a long-gone cup of cocoa.

"Hi," he whispered, "Still up, huh?"

She masked her melancholy and replied," I... had a lot of schoolwork."

Ed noticed the pile of empty lunch bags on the counter. He opened the refrigerator to check, and sighed, before pulling out sandwich makings to prepare the kids' school lunches for morning. He dug into the desk drawer, pulled out a felt marker, and tossed it to Ann.

"Make yourself useful," he requested.

She silently took the pen and started writing names on the bags.

He glanced at her again.

"Everything okay? Did your brothers give you any trouble?"

Rather than answer, she changed the subject.

"How was *your* meeting?" she asked instead.

"Fine. Great."

Ann giggled.

"What...?"

She pointed to a "My Name Is..." tag still stuck to her father's shirt. He peeled it off, blushing, wadded it up, and tossed it into the trash.

Ann spotted the card on the counter, snapped it up, and read it.

"What's... **Sawk**?"

"Single Adults with Kids—it's a single-parents' group."

"Oh..."

Ann flipped the card over, finding a name and phone number scrawled on the back. "Who's Deir...?"

Ed snatched the card back from her, answering, "Deirdre Grand, and stop being so *nosy*. Get some fruit."

Ann pulled over the fruit bowl and started examining and sorting apples, oranges, grapes, and bananas, the nicest orange going into Matty's bag, the bruisiest banana into Frank's.

Ed exchanged Matty's with a clump of grapes.

"Matty won't eat oranges," he explained. "She's a nice lady."

"Who?"

"Deirdre Grand."

"Oh?" Ann answered, casually. "Maybe you need a second opinion?"

Ed laughed.

"You mean have all you kids size her up for me?"

"No. But... maybe *one* of us whose opinion you trust?"

Ed chewed away the beginnings of a smile, folding the tops of the bags closed, and transferring them into the refrigerator.

"*Is* there one of you kids I can trust?'

"Very funny."

Ann wiped the counter and rinsed the sponge, sighing, "I'm gonna miss this ol' house."

Ed sighed back, "*Enough* for one evening, Annie."

"It's just... we all grew up here, Daddy. This is our *home.*"

Ed crossed to the light switches and turned back to her, waving her out of the kitchen.

"I don't want to talk about it anymore tonight. Okay? *Enough.* I'm tired. Now go to bed."

"Right."

Lynn Mayer, who was partnered with Ann in their Home Economics class, dumped banana slices into Ann's bowl of thickening strawberry-banana Jell-O while Ann gently folded them in.

"Remember, when you want to incorporate heavier pieces of fruit or vegetables into your gelatin molds, you wait until it is half-set. That way the added pieces will not fall to the bottom of the mold and instead will be evenly distributed throughout your dish," advised Miss Haines, the class instructor.

"While you finish up, I want to remind you about the contest," she continued.

Miss Haines, pointed to a colorful poster heralding the Future Homemakers of America competition she had just pinned up on the bulletin board at the front of the room—right next to the petition Miss Espy had been circulating, requesting the school graduate Billy Bobbs posthumously.

"The local regional contest will be held right here during your Christmas vacation, so it is entirely up to you if you want to participate, girls," she said, then corrected herself, "and Fred."

Ann carefully poured the thickening Jell-O and banana slices into an anodized aluminum mold Lynn had already lined on the outside edge with more lengthwise-sliced bananas, being careful not to dislodge any. Ann then opened their assigned refrigerator while Lynn carefully transferred it in to fully set.

"The first prize for the regional is fifty dollars— *cash*," Miss Haines continued, "and a shot at the nationals **and** a *one hundred dollar* scholarship for the college of your choice—**wow!**"

A quick knockity-knock on the classroom door was followed by a delivery man carrying a large bouquet of peach-colored roses.

"Oh, for *me?*" Miss Haines assumed, blushing.

"Is there an Ann Benjamin here?" the delivery man asked, reading his delivery slip. "Ann Benjamin...?"

Miss Haines' face fell as she pointed to Ann, who shook herself out of a stupor to slowly raise her hand.

The whole class watched in silence as the delivery man walked to the back of the classroom and presented her with the bouquet.

"Here you are, Miss Benjamin."

Thank you."

The delivery man hesitated. Ann got the hint and opened her purse to dig out and tip him a couple quarters. He left as the class murmured in excited curiosity until Miss Haines clapped her hands sharply to silence them and added, "Okay, the rose parade is over—let's get back to our burners."

Ann was at a loss. She smelled the blooms and took

a moment to just stare at them.

Who could have sent these?

There was a small envelope buried in them—Ann extracted it and tore it open to read the card inside.

"Who are they from, who are they from...?!" Lynn pressed.

I'm sorry —Frank

(Go ahead: Milk it for all it's worth.)

Ann sighed and smiled to herself while Lynn hopped up and down and flapped like a bird with impatience, finally trying to reach for the card.

"Let *me* read!"

Ann pulled it away.

"It's... *personal.*"

"Well... who sent them? ***Tell!***"

"Just a boy I know..." Ann began, buying time while developing some possible scenarios to settle on the best one, "...he's ...he's from another school. He's in *college* actually, so you wouldn't know him. His name is Maurice...."

"Sounds foreign."

"Uh-huh, he's from Manhattan. And his parents, like, own about half of it. So he's really *really* rich. And really smart. Oh, and *handsome*—kinda like Paul McCartney."

Ann paused to chuckle blithely to herself at some imaginary thought and continued with another giggle.

"The funniest thing happened over the weekend when we were on his *yacht*...."

Lynn soaked it all up like a dry sponge-cake being drenched in rum-syrup.

119

Chapter Seven

Outsiders

Ed rang the front bell—it chimed in eight note Westminster Quarters rather than simply ringing or buzzing.

He wasn't sure what to think about that.

He had decided to actually follow Ann's recommendation and bring someone with him whose opinion he trusted.

Matty peeked around his dad's leg at the plastic fern in a cast iron holder next to the front door. He imagined that there was a plastic slug named Silly-Putty who lived in its pot and left actual Saran Wrap trails.

Deirdre Grand opened the door and smiled at Ed.

"Hello!" Ed responded cheerily.

"Hi, Edward. Thank you *so much* for coming in my hour of *need*," she replied, urging them in.

Ed had a hard time walking, as Matty kept a tight grip on the back of his trouser leg.

Matty looked around the plastic-laminated, pressed-wood paneled entryway. He looked down. The floor was sheet-linoleum printed with the shapes and soft relief of colored flagstones.

Is everything here made of plastic?

He peeked around his dad's leg again, curious to see if this woman was made of plastic too.

Other than her hair, which looked more like caramel-flavored cotton candy than plastic, she seemed normal enough.

Ed reached for Matty and tried to gently but firmly wrench him around in front of him rather than behind him—but eventually gave up.

"I brought my youngest, Matty, with me. I hope you don't mind."

"Not at all. Hello, Matty!" Deirdre cooed, as she leaned down to greet him.

Matty remained mute and hidden, eyeing her cautiously from between his dad's legs.

"He's being shy," Ed explained with a chuckle.

Deirdre led them into the living room.

It was definitely a squeaky-clean, everything-in-its-place house that smelled of fake pine trees. There were plastic covers on the furniture and plastic runners on the carpets.

Matty took in the room, marveling over the many cabinets and cases and sideboards full of racks of silver spoons, painted plates in military-precision rows, and shelf after shelf of Lladro and Hummel figurines.

Matty imagined Deirdre as a witch who would cast spells on people to miniaturize them and lock them behind glass—which made both her and her house more interesting to him.

"Boy, how do you keep your house so clean?" Ed remarked. "You'll have to teach me the trick."

Matty figured she just *dinka-dinka-dee*-ed her nose like Samantha on TV.

"Tia's away at boarding school, and, well... I *cheat*," she giggled. "I have a cleaning woman. The house is simply too big for me to handle all *alone*."

Deirdre made direct eye contact with Ed on the word "alone."

He fidgeted.

"I can give you Greeta's number if you are interested."

"Um... sure," Ed replied, rubbing the back of his neck.

Matty's curiosity got the better of him and he let go of his dad's pant leg to wander off the plastic runner onto virgin beige carpet to examine a collection of various plaster and ceramic bunnies arranged in one corner of the room, wondering how Deirdre actually managed to turned them to stone.

One looked especially realistic. He reached out to touch it.

Deirdre slipped over to stop him.

"No. Those are for looking, not touching, Matty."

He gave her a second look. She had a nice smile. She didn't look like much of a witch. She was probably a boring, nice one.

He scanned the rest of her collections.

"Do you have any stone tigers?" he asked.

"No," she answered, "but I have some ceramic kitties."

"Kitties don't eat rabbits."

Deirdre gave up on the conversation to turn her attention back to Ed, motioning both of them to follow her.

"The kitchen is this way."

"Bears eat rabbits and so do lions," Matty continued, still scanning the glass cases, "Do you have any of those?"

The kitchen was just as spotless, with garden-view windows, lots of light, and more plastic flowers in pots on the windowsills.

"It was so kind of you to offer to help me on such short notice, Edward. I'm just all thumbs when it comes to anything mechanical."

While Deirdre led Ed to her stuck disposal, Matty

ran over to the sliding glass doors off of a breakfast nook to look at a clipped and highly manicured miniature apricot poodle sitting on the cement patio outside.

"No problem," Ed tossed off, "I can unstick it, I *think*. I'll need something like a broom handle."

The poodle barely moved—only enough to lock a frozen stare on Matty.

"Oh! Don't touch the windows, dear," Deirdre called out before Matty could lean in to make faces at the dog.

"Can I go outside?' Matty asked.

"Yes you can, that's a *good* place for you," Deirdre cooed, quickly stepping over to open the door for him and let him out. "You can play with Gigi!"

Deirdre helped Matty out with a firm hand at his back before closing the glass door... and latching it.

Matty examined semi-frozen Gigi.

Her head and eyes followed him eerily while her body remained motionless. He slowly waved his hand around to watch Gigi's head rotate to follow it.

He noticed a rubber toy bone at the other end of the patio and retrieved it.

Even the dog's bone is made of plastic?

He brought it back to show it to Gigi—then tossed it out onto the lawn.

Gigi's eyes darted from Matty to the bone to Deirdre through the window and back to Matty then stopped again.

"It's okay. She told me I could play with you."

Matty fetched the rubber bone instead and brought it back to show it to Gigi again. He tossed it a second time.

Nothing.

Matty gave up on the stupid dog and scanned the rest of the yard for something else to do. There were cement ducks wandering across a flower bed and a cement faun under a small tree, also staring at him.

Maybe she really is a witch after all.

He decided she must be and that Gigi must still be in the process of changing to stone. He re-approached the dog and reached out to feel her and check.

Gigi let out a low, rumbling growl and bared a fang.

Matty withdrew his hand—then tried again.

Again, Gigi growled, this time baring both fangs and her lower front teeth.

Matty withdrew. He turned his back, took two steps away from the dog—and spun on one foot to lean in, yelling, **"*Boo!*"**

Gigi vaulted into the air, as if electrified and *yipe— yipe—yipe*—ed off to the far corner of the yard to hide, quivering, behind a plastic garden shed.

Disappointed Gigi was just a normal old boring dog, and with nothing else of interest to do, Matty decided to go back inside, but the door was latched tight.

He smushed his face against the clean glass to get a better look inside.

Ed had been following Matty's antics out of the corner of his eye. He extracted the broom handle from the disposal, turned on the faucet and flipped a switch. The disposal started right up.

"Oh, Edward... thank you, I..."

Matty stared at his father, grimaced goofily, and crossed his eyes. Ed crossed his eyes and stuck out his tongue right back at him.

Deirdre's nattering stopped and Ed refocused.

"I'm sorry," Ed replied with a nervous chuckle, realizing he wasn't paying any attention to her prattle and hadn't a clue what she had just said.

"I guess it would seem funny to you. One child and I send her off to boarding school, but I'm sure with your *six* you've considered it..."

Matty, aware he had his father's attention, made more goofy faces at him against the glass while Deirdre chatted on about raising a child all on her own after losing her husband, and her many theories on proper child-rearing.

Matty pressed his nose up against the window like a pig, then flattened it the other direction.

Deirdre had her back to the window and was completely unaware of Matty's antics.

"...and I feel it is *soooo* important with children to maintain proper discipline. I'm ***very big on discipline***..." she continued.

Matty unexpectedly suction-cupped his lips to the window and blew out his cheeks like a puffer-fish, making Ed spontaneously chuckle.

Deirdre blushed and demurred, thinking Ed was laughing at what she just said.

"I meant discipline for *children*."

Matty wiggled his tongue goofily around inside his now open, balloon-like, puffer-fish mouth.

Ed burst out with a real belly laugh as Deirdre turned beet red and gasped, "Now ***really***, Edward! What kind of a woman do you think I ***am?***"

Ann felt very grown up as she drove home from St. Helena's with Matty strapped in the passenger seat next to her. Being able to drive to school and back allowed a certain feeling of freedom, despite her now having to do the shopping and errands—like dropping off and picking up Matty from St. Helena's.

126

Matty was pleased with this new arrangement because Ann could pick him up at 3:30 PM and he didn't have to wait until his dad finished work—usually all the other kids were gone by mid-afternoon and hanging out for several hours alone with a bunch of nuns was pretty much torture.

Ann pulled into the driveway to spot Randy, Tony, and Benny digging through and yanking stuff out of their row of metal trash cans. Frank rode up on his bike just as she and Matty got out of the car to see what was up.

All four trash cans were stuffed to overflowing—with their things.

"How did *this* get in here?" Benny groused, pulling out the skate board with the bent wheel he was planning to fix someday.

"And *these*?!" Randy gasped, collecting up his stack of dog-eared *MAD* magazines.

They looked at each other in confusion until they each began to remember the dinner conversation with their dad the night before. They usually only half-listened when he said things, but Ann was the first to recall dad mentioning that he had hired Deirdre's...

"The cleaning lady!" they all gasped as they raced to the front door.

They burst in together and stopped dead in their tracks, slack jawed.

The entry way and living room were starkly, *immaculately* clean.

"*Whoa*," Randy gulped.

"*Whoa*," Benny repeated as he actually saw his reflection stare back at him in the squeaky-clean floor.

They all dashed into the kitchen, which was as sterile as an operating room.

"Double *Whoa!*" Tony gasped.

Matty heard whimpering and looked over to see a humiliated Chaos sitting on the back patio... in a diaper.

"Triple *Whoa*," Matty added.

They stared at Chaos in disbelief and then back at one another for a moment... when *bing!*, a light dawned.

"*My room!*" they each squealed, except Frank, who gasped, "*My laser!*"

Frank burst into the wash room—which now looked like a tidy laundry room without any hint of his workspace or projects or tools remaining, including his laser!

"*Noooooooooo!!!!*"

Ann bolted into her now-stark room, with its empty desktop and crisply made bed. Her diary was set out on her bedside table, a pen next to it, opened to the day's date.

"*Aaaaaaaaaaaaahhh!!!*"

Matty, Benny, and Tony ran in circles around their clear floor, popping open closets and drawers to in search in vain for anything that resembled their actual room.

"*Aaaaaaaaaaaaahhh!!!*"

Randy stood frozen in the middle of his and Frank's empty, now sparklingly clean room. He opened the closet in hopes of finding everything missing there, only to find its inside as starkly clean as everything else.

He collapsed into the desk chair, put his head in his hands, and wept.

The sun was setting by the time they sorted through the trash and retrieved multiple loads of all their treasured things—miraculously, nothing was broken (that hadn't already been) and Frank's laser was completely unmolested, having been carefully placed out next to the cans in the open cardboard box he had it stored in.

The housekeeper must have been afraid enough of it to treat it like a bomb that might go off, Frank figured.

"It wouldda been better to just do our chores," Benny reluctantly admitted.

"Oh, *Daaaaddy!*" Randy mocked, aping Ann. "We need a *housekeeper!*"

Ann rolled her eyes at her own words come back to haunt her while she held the door open for her brothers and repeated in Latin, while beating a breast, "*Mea culpa, mea culpa, mea **maxima** culpa....*"

As they reached the top of the stairs the front door burst open again.

They all turned to look down.

It was their dad.

He took one look around the spotless downstairs, glanced up at them, grinned broadly, and said, "**Whoa!** Looks *great*, huh? We'll sure have to keep Greeta around!"

Ed dashed on and they heard him exclaim from the kitchen, "*Whoa!*"

The Benjamin kids all exchanged weary looks, with all eyes ending on Frank.

Frank looked back at them and narrowed his.

"Greeta's toast."

Greeta, clad in a crisp head scarf, apron, Playtex Living Gloves, and toting her waste bin and bucket full of cleaning supplies, marched up the stairs, stopping first at Matty, Benny, and Tony's room.

A crayoned note taped to the door read:

KEEP OUT!—THIS MEANS YOU!!!

It included a skull and crossbones.

Greeta snapped it down, crumpled and tossed the note into her waste bin, spritzed the door with cleaner, wiped away any residual tape adhesive, and entered their room.

She dumped bags and boxes of Matty, Benny, and Tony's stuff back into the trash cans.

Greeta's gloved hand slid around the knob to Frank and Randy's bedroom door preventing her from turning it—it had been greased. She sprayed it liberally with cleaning solvent, wiped it dry and entered their room.

She dumped Randy and Frank's junk back into the trash cans.

Greeta entered Ann's room and paused. Everything seemed as neat and tidy as she left it the last time she cleaned.

Huh...

She turned to leave but then, crossed to the closet and opened it to watch a sea of Ann's mess escape.

She dumped Ann's stuff into the cans outside.

Greeta entered the laundry room with a basket of dirty linens.

A narrow passage to the washer and dryer had been cordoned off with hazard tape and cones. Frank's reestablished workspace was guarded by a wild mesh of bare electrical wire behind "WARNING" signs and more hazard tape. Red lights flashed and soft beepers sounded. "DANGER" and "HIGH VOLTAGE" signs hung over Frank's worktable.

Greeta set her load of laundry on top of the dryer, removed her rubber gloves, and, arms akimbo, assessed the situation.

She went outside to the fuse box to shut off the main power switch.

She returned to the now silent, dark, and disarmed room. She stepped past the safety cones, pulled down the tape and signs, and climbed through a gap in the mesh of now-dead wires.

A large empty box sat under the table—the perfect thing to collect Frank's mess in. Greeta lifted it.

She heard a faint "click."

She paused, shook it off, and, not noticing nor grasping the significance of the rows of batteries wired in series and Frank's Model T coil all connected up beneath the table, began placing his tools and things into the box.

She reached over to take down the wire mesh as electricity crackled through her body.

The phone rang during dinner and Ed heard an ocean of rage, some of it in German, pour from Greeta. The Benjamin kids listened, ears cocked, while eating mechanically so as not to appear to be eavesdropping.

"Well, she **quit!**" Ed roared. "Are you all *happy?!*"

The kids tried with all their might *not* to look thrilled.

Ed glanced at Randy, who was straining to make a real tear run down his cheek.

"Nice try."

Ed returned to his seat at the table, folded his hands, and leaned in.

"I'll give you kids only one more chance to make this housekeeper thing work or you'll be back on your own."

It was mid-afternoon when Matty and Ann returned home. Oddly, the front door was unlocked. The last kid out must have forgotten, Ann figured.

"Better not let Dad know," Ann told Matty. "He'd be really angry."

They entered. The air seemed fresher than usual for a closed up house. Ann couldn't shake the feeling that something was definitely off. She looked about; a couple of windows had been left open too.

Weird.

Ann started upstairs to take her books to her room.

Meanwhile, Matty stepped out in the back yard to

132

play and found a strange child his own age he had never seen before sitting in the middle of a planting bed of bare dirt, licking a stick. A filthy teddy bear with a muddy face sat next to the boy.

The kid hummed to himself, taking no notice of Matty.

Matty watched the kid roll his spittle-stick in the dust to coat it, then lick the clinging dirt from it like it was a mud-popsicle.

Ann tossed her schoolbooks and tote on her bed and crossed the hall to use the bathroom. When she opened the door she was startled to find a strange woman inside taking a bubble bath.

"Oh, 'scuse me," Ann blurted without thinking, closing the door.

She stood in the hallway a moment, utterly confused. She knocked.

"Um... excuse me?" Ann yelled through the door, "Who *are* you?"

"Be out in a minute!" the unknown woman chirped back.

Back out in the yard, Matty had been joined by Benny. Both watched the weird kid hum indecipherable tunes while eating mudsicles made from his own spit, which he periodically shared with his teddy bear. The weird kid completely froze every so often to stare off into space, then giggle about something to himself before going back to making and eating more mud.

Tony soon joined them and, after taking in the odd tableau for several minutes, asked," Who *is* he?"

Tony's brothers shrugged.

Benny turned to the boy.

"Hey, kid. Who are you?"

"Willy!" the kid answered in a giggle without looking at them, as if talking to himself rather than them, while remaining completely focused on his mud stick.

"He's Willy," Benny repeated to his brothers with another shrug.

Ann leaned against the wall outside the bathroom door until the woman emerged, wrapped in a bath towel with a second towel turbaned around her head.

Before Ann could confront her, the woman smiled cheerily at her while trotting down the hall and said, "Oh, hi! You must be Ann. I'm Linda, the new housekeeper? Excuse me a sec, hon—I need to get dressed."

Linda slipped into the master bedroom and locked the door, leaving Ann in slack-jawed disbelief.

When the Benjamins all sat down to fried chicken, mashed potatoes and gravy, and buttered peas, Ed remarked how nice the house looked.

"Daddy, where did you find this new housekeeper?" Ann asked.

"From that big bulletin board in the supermarket."

"No wonder."

"What now," he laughed, dropping his fork with a clank. "You don't approve of free advertising? The house looks good—not *Greeta* good, but better than you kids ever kept it."

"But... you don't know *anything* about her," Ann argued. "Don't you think it would be safer to go through an agency?"

134

"I know she's a single mother trying to make her way in the world. And I know the house is clean—that's all I need to know. So you kids just stay away from her when she's here working. I don't want you screwing it up again."

"Don't look at me," Frank said, playing innocent.

"Her kid is a weirdo," Benny informed.

"Totally," Tony confirmed.

"He eats dirt," Matty added.

"You boys be nice to him," Ed scolded. "He lost his father."

Randy gaped, about to point out the obvious irony in his dad's scold, but thinking better of it remained mute.

"Daddy..." Ann started, sounding firm, "...I *think* I should tell you..."

Ed dropped his fork again.

"Ann, whatever it is I don't want to hear it!"

"*FINE!*"

"Don't raise your voice at me, young lady!" Ed scolded. "You're the one who insisted we need a housekeeper, so you just *better* make it work—because this is your last chance!"

"I said fine," Ann mumbled back.

All ate in silence. Ed took a second helping of chicken.

"Your fried chicken is really good, Annie," he said, trying to ease the mood.

"Linda made it," Randy corrected.

"*Really?!*" Ed perked. "She's a good cook too—hey, that's *great!*"

Ann got up with a curt, "Excuse me, I have homework," and cleared her place, then left the room.

Ann slammed her bedroom door, locked it, and flopped onto her bed to scream into her pillow.

When she felt sufficiently screamed out she dug between her mattresses for her diary to write it all down. She couldn't reach it so she got down next to the bed to dig deeper.

Still no diary.

She lifted her side of the mattress. Nothing there. She scrambled over to the other side of her bed and lifted that.

There it was.

On the wrong side of the bed?

She pulled it out.

The latch was loose.

"*Linda!*"

Ann pulled up to the house. Linda's car was in the middle of the driveway, hogging the whole thing, so she parked at the curb.

Matty undid his seatbelt. He looked back at Linda's car and then at Ann. She didn't undo her seatbelt.

"I'll be at the library," she told Matty.

He climbed out of the car and watched her drive away before scampering into the house.

Linda was banging around in the kitchen while the radio blared rock tunes, so Matty wandered up to his bedroom. He found Benny, seated on Tony's bed, watching Willy. The weird kid was giggling and spinning in tight circles in the center of the room, while staring at the ceiling.

136

Benny eyed the second hand on the alarm clock next to Tony's bed.

"He's been doing that for... six minutes and forty-three seconds," Benny explained.

Down in the garage, Randy, Tony, and several neighborhood kids watched Frank check the glue on some arrow feathers he had attached to the handle of a toilet plunger, making it look like a giant ACME suction-cup dart from a Road Runner cartoon.

Randy waited with their homemade crossbow.

"Ready?" Randy asked.

"Ready," Frank confirmed, as they all marched to the back yard to test it out.

An old metal oil drip pan had been nailed to the fence between their yard and the Coe's. Tony took the hose and wet the surface of the pan and then Frank wet the plunger on the arrow.

Frank cranked back the crossbow string, took ten paces back, loaded the arrow in the bow, aimed, and fired.

The arrow hit the pan with a loud, soggy *clang*... and stuck tight.

The neighborhood kids let out a rousing cheer and applause as Ross peeked through a crack in the fence, trying to figure out *what-the-heck* was going on.

"My turn," Randy claimed as he popped the plunger loose and re-wet both it and the metal tray.

He paced off his distance, cranked back the bow string as far as he could, loaded the arrow, aimed, and fired.

His aim was too high.

"Oops."

The plunger sailed right over the fence into the Coe's back yard.

137

They heard a dull smack and an "*Ooof!*" followed by a thud.

A dozen heads popped over the top of the fence to see Ross splayed out on his back patio, squealing like a pig, their cartoon arrow rolling back and forth on its cup next to him.

"Ross-Coe, Bosco, Ross-Coe, Bosco...!" the kids all laughed and chanted as Ross dashed into his house in tears.

Up in the master bedroom, Linda dusted a bureau. She went to move a small covered basket which was surprisingly heavy. She opened it and discovered a stash of spare change. Linda looked about, went over to the door, latched it, and returned to the bureau. She sorted through the change, selecting out most of the dimes, quarters, and half-dollars, leaving the pennies and nickels and one or two quarters at the top to mask her theft and replaced the covered basket. She scraped the coins off the edge of the dresser into her hand and slipped them into her pocket. She tossed her dust rag in her cleaning supplies bucket and turned on the vacuum cleaner.

While the vacuum stood running in place... she snooped further.

Ed's closet was full of all his clothes—nothing left of his wife's to be of any interest to her. The dresser drawers were the same—all his.

Linda scanned the room and fixed her eyes on the large cedar chest at the end of the bed.

That looks promising.

She crossed to *creak* it open.

Removing an extra chenille bedspread she found Ellen's old keepsakes stored beneath: photographs of ancestors, of younger Ellen and Ed, of all the kids, a stack of homemade Mother's Day and Birthday cards, a box of old dry corsages, *lots* of baby shoes with labels, and a stack of beautiful hand-tatted lace linens—a large tablecloth, a table runner, and several lace doilies.

"Pretty."

Underneath the laces at the bottom of the chest sat a jewelry box. Linda dug it out and opened it up.

It was full of mostly understated costume jewelry: a thin string of faux pearls, various sets of clip-on earrings. She tried a few on.

Hmm...

There was a smaller velvet-covered box tucked deeper inside. Linda opened it to reveal a Deco-style platinum broach with a vivid rectangular emerald at its center surrounded by baguette-cut diamonds.

"*Ooooh!*"

Linda polished it on her apron and held it up to see it sparkle in the light.

A very dizzy Willy collapsed to the floor giggling. Benny checked the clock.

"Twelve minutes and fourteen seconds that time," he remarked.

"Jeez," Matty huffed, "What a goof."

"Willy fall down!" Willy laughed. He staggered back to his feet. There was a brief moment where he stood frozen, gape-mouthed, and unblinking, before he began giggling and spinning again.

"Do you think he'll throw up?" Matty wondered.

Benny shrugged while noting the time again.

Willy spun and giggled and giggled and spun. The more he spun the wilder his circular path became—his erratic steps landing closer and closer to Matty's toy box and his favorite toy Tonka truck, which he had neglected to put away.

Matty leapt up too late to save it—Willy's foot stomped the truck's cab, shattering the plastic windshield and crumpling the top flat, and in the process tripping himself to the floor in a fit of giggles.

Matty rescued what was left of his truck, holding back tears.

Benny grabbed Willy by the collar and shoved his face at the squashed truck.

"Look what you did, you stupid little creep!" Benny yelled.

"Willy not do that, Willy not do that..." Willy denied repeatedly, shaking his head between fits of giggles.

Benny held Willy while Matty prepared to punch him in the face, but then reconsidered. Spying Willy's teddy bear off in the corner of the room, he snatched it up and shook it in front of Willy's face.

Willy stopped giggling and stared, gape-mouthed at the bear.

Matty placed his hands tightly around the bear's neck and squeezed with all his might.

Willy let out a blood-curdling, window-shattering screech.

Linda shoved Benny and Matty out the front door and locked it. They kicked and pounded and multi-rang the doorbell, but Linda ignored them. They were interrupted by Mrs. Coe marching up their walkway, holding the toilet plunger arrow while wearing plastic gloves so she wouldn't have to touch it.

"This is not a toy!" she snarled at them and then tried with all her might to break the arrow over her knee in front of them. But the wooden dowel was far too thick and wouldn't give, so she slammed it onto the concrete porch instead.

"Thanks, Mrs. Coe?" offered Benny.

"Don't you brats get funny with me or you'll get more than you bargained for!" she threatened, and stomped off.

"She didn't say, 'you're welcome,'" Matty noted. "That's not very polite."

Benny shrugged. He picked up the plunger arrow.

"Cool arrow though. Wonder where she got it?"

"And why she gave it to us?"

Linda frosted a Duncan Hines chocolate layer cake she had baked for the Benjamin's dessert.

Willy sat on the counter next to her, hugging his teddy bear and licking the beater, chocolate frosting smeared all over his face.

He smushed the beater into the bear's face, coating it in frosting too.

"Willy feed Teddy," he giggled.

Linda finished frosting. She pulled a paper plate and Saran Wrap out of the cupboard and, cutting the cake in two, put the bigger half onto the paper plate and gently wrapped it in Saran.

She set it next to other plates of the Benjamin's food she had prepared and packed for herself and Willy to take home with them.

She quickly washed the last of the dishes, wiped Willy, the teddy bear, and the kitchen counter clean before announcing, "Okay, Willy. Time to go home."

"Willy go home?"

"Yes, honey—Willy go home."

Ann pulled up to the front of the house and had to park at the curb again because Linda's car was *still* hogging the whole driveway. She jumped out and approached Benny and Matty, who were tossing the suction-cup arrow at Linda's windshield, trying to make it stick.

"Try wetting it," Matty suggested.

Benny ran down to dip it in the gutter.

"Linda's *still* here?" Ann growled.

"She locked us out," Matty explained.

"She... **WHAT?!**" Ann roared.

Ann jingled her keys at her little brothers.

"Come on!"

They reached the front door just as Linda exited with Willy and her grocery bag of stolen food. She didn't expect to see Ann.

Linda tried to step around her, but Ann got right in her face.

"What gives you the right to lock *my* brothers out of *our* house?!"

"They were picking on my Willy," Linda shot back.

Linda brushed past Ann and the boys headed to her car—as she did her coat splayed open and Ann got a glimpse of something familiar pinned to Linda's blouse.

Ann pursued, spun Linda, and grabbed her coat,

142

pulling it open to reveal the broach.

"That's my mother's!" Ann screamed. "You **thief!** Give it back!"

Ann grabbed for the broach. Linda dropped her bag and let go of Willy's hand to defend herself. The two tussled, but Ann was able to grab the broach, ripping Linda's blouse wide open to free it.

Willy loosed his piercing, glass-shattering screech again.

Linda came back at Ann, readying to strike her, but Ann slapped Linda hard across her face first, startling her.

Linda backed off.

"You're insane!" Linda defended, holding her stinging cheek, wrapping her coat around her torn blouse, and pulling Willy to her side, "I've had that broach for years!"

Matty and Benny looked in the bag before Linda snatched it back from them.

"Don't make me *hurt* you!" Ann snarled, re-approaching Linda, both fists clenched.

"Get in the car, Willy," Linda ordered and they both climbed in. Linda locked the car doors.

Ann pounded on her window as Linda pulled out, yelling, "Don't you **ever** come back here—you hear me! You're **fired!**"

Benny lofted the plunger arrow and with an angry toss nailed it to the back window of Linda's car as she sped off.

Ed got the call at work—the one where Linda told *her* side of the story: how the boys cruelly picked on her son and how Ann physically attacked her and tore her blouse.

143

He came home to find Ann locked in her bedroom crying. By the time he popped the latch and stood in the doorway to yell at her he was beyond angry and Ann was sobbing so hard she couldn't speak.

"You should be *ashamed* of yourself!" Ed scolded. "You're worse than the boys! You're not to come out of this room until you call Linda and apologize!"

Ed slammed Ann's door, stomped into his bedroom, and slammed his own.

The Benjamin boys flinched at the sounds of the slamming. Frank went back to helping Benny with his math homework.

Matty was hiding under the kitchen table, furiously drawing on the underside of it with his crayons.

Randy stood vigil by the window eyeing the Coe's house.

"Maybe she won't do anything this time," Randy suggested.

"Don't bet on it," Frank countered.

Tony wandered over to the TV to see if there was anything worth watching until dinner. He noticed a lace doily now sat on top of it. He picked it up to examine it.

A door opened upstairs followed by his father's footfalls on the stairs.

"Okay, boys. Get washed for dinner." Ed yelled upstairs, "Ann! Supper!"

Tony nodded and set the doily back on the TV. As he moved to follow his brothers out Ed crossed to the TV and picked up the doily, grabbing Tony's arm.

"Who put this here?" he asked.

"I dunno," Tony shrugged. "Linda, I guess."

Ed entered the kitchen, still holding the doily. The table was adorned with a lace tablecloth and set for dinner. The boys all entered and sat in their places. Frank noticed the tablecloth and the doily in his dad's hand.

He recognized them.

Ann entered the room, shot her father an angry look, crossed to his place at the table, and slammed down the broach.

"*This* was pinned to her blouse."

Ann crossed to the phone.

She dialed.

"Hello? Is this Linda?" Ann asked.

Ed looked at the broach. He dropped the doily, crossed to the phone, and took it from Ann.

"Hello, Linda?" Ed growled into the receiver. "This is Ed Benjamin. You're fired!"

He hung up the phone and Ann slipped to her seat. Ed followed and they all said grace.

Ed noticed that half the cake was missing. He would normally blame the kids, but... he pointed to the cake and asked Benny, "Linda?"

"Linda," he affirmed.

Matty examined the tablecloth with fascination.

"Where'd this come from?" he asked.

"It was your mother's," Ed explained. "Her mother made it."

Ed sighed.

"It's Ann's now."

Ed got up and handed the broach to Ann.

"As is... *this*."

Ann and her father exchanged contrite smiles.

The phone rang.

"I got it!" Randy volunteered, jumping up.

But his dad got there first.

"Hello? Oh, Mrs. Coe—*yes?* No...? They... **WHAT?!**"

Mr. and Mrs. White strolled past the Benjamin's house on their evening constitutional to hear Ed yelling, his kids yelling back, doors slamming, spanking noises, and kids crying.

"There go the Benjamins again," Mr. White sighed, giving his wife a concerned glance.

"They must have all driven that poor woman to her grave, God rest her soul," Mrs. White sighed back.

Chapter Eight

Thanks, But No Thanks

What sparked Ann's idea was her home-ec teacher, Miss Haines', homework assignment to "Plan the Ideal Thanksgiving Meal."

Thanksgiving had always been her mother's favorite holiday, which meant Ann had great recipes to draw on for her assignment, and she aced it. Since Ellen's death, it was hard to find many things for the Benjamins to be thankful for. Like Christmas, Thanksgiving didn't really exist for them anymore.

Ann's hope was to change that, so she resolved to actually prepare her ultimate Thanksgiving meal for the family this year—with all the favorite dishes her mom used to serve. The kind of meal that couldn't help but make all of them remember the good times. To want to be a *family* again. Since this was likely the last Thanksgiving they would spend together in this house, and her last one before she would be going off to college, she was determined to make it a *perfect* one.

Ann bought some autumnal-colored paisley fabric, took out her mother's old Singer, and, secretly, in her bedroom at night, began sewing a new tablecloth and napkins for the big event.

Occasionally one of her brothers would pass her room and hear the sounds of the sewing machine, but none paid any attention, figuring Ann was just doing "girl's stuff."

When Thanksgiving Day finally came though, Benny spent most of it brooding about some unknown injustice or another each of his brothers and the world in general had done to him. Ann was usually the one to talk him through these things and sort it all out with him, but she had to focus on the meal, so he was left on his own to wallow in his private misery.

Matty spent the morning wandering around the back yard poking things with a stick and then the rest of the afternoon under the kitchen table making drawings or lying on his back staring up at its underside, ignoring Ann as she prepared the meal, decorated and set the table, and generally tidied up.

Frank and Randy were out in the back yard all afternoon trying to ignite the sample chunk of solid rocket fuel their dad had brought home from work that week using everything from a magnifying glass to a propane torch. They were, thankfully, unsuccessful, but only because Frank's laser was not yet fully functional.

Tony was missing, having left earlier in the day, freshly showered and smelling of Old Spice.

And after he pounded a "For Sale by Owner" sign in the front lawn, Ed spent the rest of the day trying in vain to spruce up his homely Nova—washing, waxing, polishing, vacuuming the interior—which all started and then snowballed because he simply needed to replace a dead tail light. But he figured if he was going to seriously start dating again, he needed nicer-looking wheels. His efforts didn't do very much good for the poor old dented thing, and by the time he finished it, the best one could say was that it seemed the bulk of the filth from the car had simply migrated onto him.

Ann stuck her head out from the front door and called out, "Dinner, Daddy!"

Ann's table tableau could have been a November cover for *Good Housekeeping*. Her freshly sewn harvest-colored linens provided the stage, graced by a horn of plenty centerpiece, set with the good Franciscan Apple ware and their grandmother's polished silver.

Then... the family arrived.

Her still-filthy dad had only bothered to wash his hands before sitting down to Ann's fancy dinner.

Matty needed to be sent back to the bathroom to clean up his still messy paws.

Benny sulked in and slouched down next to Frank, who started to reach for some food.

"Wait for grace, Frank," Ann ordered.

"Yeah, Frank." Her father seconded.

"Where's Tony?" Ann noticed the empty chair.

"At his *girlfriend's* house," Randy snarked.

"He'll miss dinner," Ann huffed.

"No, he won't. He said he's gonna eat with *her* family," Randy explained.

Ann stared at the empty chair.

"More for us," Ed stated. "C'mon, Annie. Let's eat."

Ed quickly led them through grace and started carving the bird.

Ann waited for it. Would they recognize their mother's touch?

No. Not an ounce of nostalgic recognition, or even a "thank you" or compliment was uttered.

Even after they all ate her perfectly roasted turkey, their mother's rye-bread, giblet, diced dried apricot, and toasted pine nut stuffing, fluffy mashed potatoes, carrots, and onions topped with mushroom and giblet gravy, candied yams, homemade blood orange/cranberry sauce, a green salad sprinkled with bacon bits and toasted pumpkin seeds, and, in Ann's own humble opinion, the best pumpkin pies topped with heavy whipping cream she had *ever* made.

149

The meal was almost eaten in silence.

Oh, they all scarfed the food down eagerly enough, noisily too, in fact none of them hardly stopped to take a breath, which was a tacit compliment, Ann supposed, but no *verbal* kudos were tossed her way. And if they thought about their mother or felt any family togetherness or nostalgic memories, they weren't sharing it.

Of course, Ann had told no one but her diary of her grand hopes for the meal; that it would somehow magically bring the family together as a unit again, the way her mother's meals always had before.

Instead, it was like there were six separate, isolated people rather than a single family sitting at her table. No one seemed to notice each other or remark how special the meal was, or compliment her beautiful linens and decorations, or even acknowledge the *massive* amount of work she had put into preparing it all for them.

Nor did any of them notice when Ann excused herself after dessert to go straight up to her room to pout and then rant about it to her diary.

Ann heard her dad call, "Family meeting!" from the living room.

She tucked her diary away and reluctantly came down to gather with her siblings while Ed stood at the hearth looking serious.

"Whatever it is, *I* didn't do it," Frank told his dad right off as he entered, toweling his hands. "I just scrubbed all the pots and pans, by the way. On Thanksgiving! That should count for something, right?" He turned to his sister. "You sure left a big mess, Ann."

She stuck out her tongue at him.

150

"Benny—he did it," Randy offered, sacrificing his little brother up to their dad's wrath even though he had no idea what any of them had actually done wrong yet.

"Nuht-uh!" Benny countered.

"Did what...?" Ann asked Benny, poking him. "What did you do *now*, Benny?!"

"Nothing!"

"Could you all hold on and let me talk here?" Ed interjected.

"I was *gone* all day, so don't look at *me!*" Tony proclaimed.

"I don't see why *I* should even be here," Ann complained. "It's not fair! You always get mad at *me* when one of *them* does something stupid!"

"I'm not mad at anybody!" Ed hollered.

"It's a good thing you're not mad, otherwise you might start yelling," Randy snarked.

Ed glared at him.

"The reason for this family meeting is... I have to go out of town on business for a few weeks. I couldn't get out of it, *believe* me, I **tried**," Ed explained, rubbing his neck and sighing. He gave his kids a stern look. "And I'm counting on you all to *behave yourselves* while I'm gone."

The Benjamin kids exchanged looks of surprise that quickly morphed into looks of enthusiasm.

"Oh, you can totally trust us," Frank promised.

"As long as I'm **completely** in charge," Ann demanded. "Daddy, tell them they all **have** to obey me while you're gone."

"No way!" Randy countered.

"*I'll* be in charge of *me*," Frank stated.

Me too!" Matty agreed.

"You're too little," Benny argued to Matty.

"I say democracy—one *man*, one *vote!*" Tony proposed.

"That leaves you women out," Randy commented to Ann, laughing.

"Daddy, will you **please** explain to these **children** that I'll be in charge while you're gone and that they **have** to listen to **me**?!" Ann insisted.

Ed shot up a stern hand to silence all of them.

"**None** of you will be in charge," he answered, "because I've already hired a sitter."

Their looks of enthusiasm melted into looks of horror.

"A *sitter*?!" they all moaned.

"Really, Daddy!" Ann complained.

"Don't worry, Annie," Ed countered. "The personnel department at work gave me her agent's name. She's *very* professional. And she'll cook and clean and take care of everything while I'm gone."

"We're too old for a sitter!" Tony insisted.

"We can take care of ourselves!" Benny countered.

"We always do anyway," Randy mumbled.

"Her name is Missus Hatchfield, and you kids are all to obey her," he explained. "Do you hear what I'm saying? What she says *goes*! Now, I want all of you to promise me you won't give her any trouble—if you do, she'll have my number, and there'll be hell to pay if she has to call me, you better believe that!"

All the kids moaned.

"So let's hear it," Ed commanded. "I promise to mind Missus Hatchfield!"

"Okay—fine!" Ann conceded while crossing her fingers behind her back.

152

"Mmm-hmm," Frank mumbled back.

"Yeah, I guess," Tony grumbled.

"I promise," Benny sighed.

"Me too," Matty whined.

"Seig heil," Randy said as he Nazi-saluted his dad.

Ed glared at him.

"Okay, okay! Geez! I **promise**!" he relented.

There was a slight pause as everyone processed their dad's news, then Randy asked the question on everyone's mind:

"So... what's this Hatchfield lady *like*?"

When Mrs. Hatchfield entered the house no one was sure *what* to think of her, including Ed.

She resembled a too-old-for-the-role local-theater version of Mary Poppins, complete with a silk flower topped hat held on by an actual hatpin. Her dress was a mauve, loose fitting, button-front, mid-calf length, out-of-date style popular in the 1940's. She wore flat, sensible shoes, and carried an alligator shoulder bag. She was a large woman and might easily have been mistaken for a man masquerading as a woman, save for her ample bosom that reached down to her lowest rib.

"Which of you young gentlemen is going to bring in my luggage for me?" she asked through a yellow-toothed smile.

Ed turned to his boys, "Frank, Randy, Tony: fetch Mrs.Hatchfield's bags."

The boys seemed frozen by the sight of her.

"NOW!" Ed barked.

Frank, Randy, and Tony quickly returned, each toting one of Mrs. Hatchfield's suitcases. They set them in the entry while the rest of the kids stood assessing this odd woman that their father's workplace had somehow deemed worthy of supervising them.

"Thank you, boys," Mrs. Hatchfield said, a little too sweetly.

"Okay, guys, don't just leave them there—take 'em up to my room," Ed ordered. "Missus Hatchfield will be staying in there while I'm gone."

Matty entered with Lugee and Chaos bounded in after him.

"Matty, no! Get the dog!" Ed started.

Too late—Chaos was at Mrs. Hatchfield's feet, tail wagging madly, licking at her and peeing in a frenzy of doggie ecstasy.

Without missing a beat, Mrs. Hatchfield reached in her alligator bag, pulled out a wad of tissues, and dropped it on the pee, then mopped it with her foot, unrattled.

"Ann, will you take care of *that*, please," Ed requested, pointing to Chaos and the pee.

Ann grabbed Chaos's collar and pulled him out of the room to quickly return with more paper towels.

There was a honk outside.

"That's my cab," Ed exhaled, checking his watch and handing Mrs. Hatchfield keys and various notes and instructions he had written out for her.

"Here's where I'll be staying and the various phone numbers where I can be reached. If anyone calls about buying the house take a number and tell them I'll call them after I return. There's our doctor's number, in case of any emergency—I've already alerted him so he can handle anything in my absence."

A second honk sounded outside as Frank, Randy,

and Tony came back down the stairs to join with the others.

"The kids all start their Christmas holiday next week," Ed continued, talking more quickly. "They've been told not to be under foot."

"Not to worry, Mister Benjamin," she replied, "I love kids and kids love me."

He gave each of the kids a quick warning glare.

"Don't you worry about a thing," Mrs. Hatchfield continued, chuckling. "I've been through it all before."

"I'm sure you have."

Randy started to help his dad with his suitcase, but Ed took it from him.

"I've got it. You kids mind yourselves, now. Remember... you *promised*."

"*Good bye*, Dad!" his kids all replied with sarcastic smiles and waves.

Ed trotted off to the street, got into the cab, waved once more from the window, and was off, while his kids and Mrs. Hatchfield waved back to him from the front porch.

Ann looked at Mrs. Hatchfield, took a deep breath, and reminded herself that she was now an adult so she should try to behave like one and set an example for her brothers.

She approached Mrs. Hatchfield, forced a smile, and extended a hand.

"Hi. I'm Ann."

Mrs. Hatchfield stared at Ann's extended hand.

She popped opened her purse, extracted a cigarette, lit it, took a deep drag followed by another French inhale and responded, "Save the soft-soap, girlie. If you think this next three weeks will be a pleasure cruise you're sorely mistaken."

Mrs. Hatchfield glanced about making eye-contact

with each of the kids, adding, "And as for the rest of you vermin, I have a number to call and I won't hesitate to use it."

Gruffly shoeing an errant kitten out of her path with a, "Put this animal outside, where it belongs," she marched up the stairs, leaving a trail of smoke marking her path into the master bedroom, where the door closed and the lock clicked shut.

"Let's hose her down and see if she melts," Randy suggested.

"Quit joking, Randy," Ann snapped back, "this looks serious."

She turned to Frank and asked, "Frank... what do you think?"

The others drew nearer while Frank contemplated.

"The Bugs Bunny philosophy," he decided.

The others looked confused.

"We don't do anything until we're provoked," Frank explained, "but the minute we are, it means **war**."

Randy got home, entered the kitchen, and plopped his books on the table while singing a new song he learned in the schoolyard.

"Suff-o-cation, takes coordination—suff-o-cation, a game we all can play..."

Frank stood by the phone, listening to the receiver. Randy noticed that Frank had unscrewed and removed the mouthpiece from the phone. Matty was at his side, holding the microphone from Frank's tape recorder for him, which sat on the desk next to them.

Randy could faintly hear what sounded like Mrs.

Hatchfield's voice on the upstairs phone. He stepped past Matty and Frank to get to the refrigerator, continuing his song while creating a Dagwood sandwich out of whatever handy he could find there.

"...First you take a plastic bag, then you place it on your head, go to bed—wake up dead, Ooooooooooh..."

He stepped past his brothers again while repeating his morbid ditty on his way to the living room to watch *The Dating Game.*

He stopped cold with his sandwich half-way to his open mouth.

There was now an empty space where their TV should have been.

He scanned the room, looked around the corner... it was gone!

"Wha-the...?" he mumbled through a mouthful of sandwich.

Randy returned to the kitchen as Frank started the tape recorder and nodded to Matty, who held the microphone up to the phone receiver, recording the call.

"Where's the teevee?!" Randy asked.

"*Shhhhh,*" Matty whispered back, lofting a finger to his lips.

Frank pointed to the microphone. Randy reluctantly clammed up and took another bite of his sandwich while pantomiming his query again. Frank dragged him into the living room while Matty continued recording.

"Okay, where's the teevee?" Randy whispered.

"Hatchetface took it up to *her* room," Frank whispered back, pointing upstairs.

"Okay! ***That's*** it!" Randy ranted in barely a whisper, "I'm provoked! Bugs Bunny time! It's ***war***—she's ***history!***"

"Too early," Frank whispered back, shaking his head.

"No it's not!" Randy argued back.

Frank pointed to Randy's sandwich.

"Just eat that and listen to me," he countered. "If we fight now, we'll lose. Trust me."

"I say we call a family meeting and vote!"

Frank calmly curled a finger at Randy urging him back into the kitchen where Matty continued to record Mrs. Hatchfield's phone conversation.

"Randy," Frank whispered to him while he adjusted some knobs on the recorder. "What do adults always tell us kids to do, or we'll fail?"

Randy shrugged, annoyed.

"Our homework," Frank answered, pointing to the spool of tape slowly revolving around, catching Mrs. Hatchfield's every word.

He placed a hand on Matty's shoulder and continued in a whisper to both of them. "Find out everything we can about her. Know her weaknesses. Let her think she's in control for a while. Play the victim. Then, when she finally crosses the line, we annihilate her."

Randy stared at his older brother, gape-mouthed.

"Do I shock you?" Frank asked.

"No," Randy whispered back while offering him a bite of his sandwich, "I'm impressed!"

Meanwhile upstairs, Mrs. Hatchfield continued her phone conversation while sprawled out on Ed's bed, propped up on pillows, in a room dense with stale smoke. The TV sat in the corner opposite her, playing *The Secret Storm*. A half-spent cigarette stuck to her lower lip kept time like a conductor's baton as she prattled on.

"...and so I says, 'I have a number to call, and I won't hesitate to use it.' I know. *I know!* Piece of cake. And when I think of Marge stuck with that quadriplegic out in Landers."

She brayed a smoker's laugh that ended in a wet, lung-shredding cough. She dropped her butt in a coffee cup on the bedside table and extracted a chocolate from a nearly demolished Whitman's Sampler on the bed next to her, popping it into her mouth.

"I keep 'em scared—works every time. What's *that*...? Because he was desperate dearie! He asked my price, I gave it—*per kid*—and he's paying through the teeth times six! 'Course the agency thinks I'm getting about half that much. Don't I know it. Ten percent and we do all the work!"

She let out a guttural guffaw, then listened while she lit another cigarette and took a deep drag.

"You said it, sister. I have this fantasy. I call him up and say, 'Harry, this is Bea Hatchfield, and for the past eight years I've only claimed *half* of what I've earned. So what are you gonna do about it?' I know! *I know...!*"

The Benjamin kids said their amens after grace while Mrs. Hatchfield stood by holding a pot and waiting for them to finish.

She circled the table three times scooping and plopping equal portions of beets, liver, and Brussel sprouts on each kid's plate before serving herself in the same manner. She sat at the head of the table and began dissecting her slab of overcooked liver. She eventually looked up to see the kids all staring at their plates in disbelief.

"Eat it now or for breakfast," Mrs. Hatchfield croaked. "Your choice."

Benny spit his fifth Brussel sprout into the toilet and flushed.

"Bleeck."

He rinsed his mouth and opened the door as silently as possible to step out of the bathroom and past the closed master bedroom door. He could hear *Bewitched* playing on the TV and cursed Mrs. Hatchfield under his breath because he had finished his homework and if she hadn't stolen the TV he normally could have been watching it.

Figures a witch like her would watch a show about witches.

He quietly slipped into his, Matty, and Tony's room, and closed and latched the door behind him.

Frank, Randy, Tony, and Matty were already seated in a circle on the floor waiting.

Benny took his place with them.

There was a noise at the window and Ann slid it open from the outside, handing in several McDonald's bags and a tray of drinks to Frank before climbing in herself.

Matty stared hungrily at the bags Frank placed in the center of the circle and crossed himself.

Ann and Frank doled out burgers, fries, and shakes all around. Everyone scarfed in silent bliss until Randy paused to breathe and took the opportunity to mock Ann with a, "Why don't you go through an *agency*, Daddy...?"

Tony and Benny laughed.

"I just got the food," Ann shot back. "So eat up and *shut up*."

Once they finished eating and Randy had removed all the incriminating evidence back through the window, across the roof, and down to the trash cans, the kids decided to play a round of hearts.

This time Ann wanted to play, so Matty was on his own.

He struggled a bit and it wasn't clear if he had a full grasp of the game yet, as he collected a pile of hearts.

"Shit!"

"Matty!" Ann scolded.

"Sorry—*shoot*."

Ann was about to try to help him but he balked, raising a palm at her.

"I can do it! Let me *do it*!"

Matty hung his head and studied his card. He looked pretty confused and pulled at his hair. He hesitated, then finally led with the ace of spades. Frank grinned and gave Matty the queen of spades. Randy followed with a jack of hearts and the others piled on their high hearts.

"You're rackin' up the points there, junior," Randy smirked.

"Uh-huh..." Matty replied, more calmly now, as he scooped the cards into his pile and calculated in his head.

"Matty...?" Ann questioned, with a glance at Frank.

Matty smiled and threw down the ace of hearts.

"You're shooting the moon?!" Ann gasped.

"Shot," he replied.

Two more quick rounds and it was all over—Matty had successfully shot the moon.

His siblings were all struck dumb.

"Twenty-six points for you and you and you and you and you: *tsk, tsk*," Matty gloated.

161

Ann sat agape, Frank stewed, Tony replayed the round in his head, and Benny snorted.

"Amazing!" Randy said, and burst out laughing.

"He got lucky," Frank decided.

"Not luck," Matty shot back, "Bugs Bunny." Matty counted on his fingers, "Find their weakness, play the victim, annihilate the opponent."

Ann's eyes popped and everyone turned to glare at Frank.

Frank paled.

"I've created a monster."

Several days passed with the Benjamin kids living under the thumb of Mrs. Hatchfield's rule. They still had school for escape, but when they were at home she treated them like her slaves, barking orders, and having them wait on her hand and foot. It was very much like them being on their own, cleaning house and doing all the same chores, but with a giant demanding baby-woman to care for on top of it all.

Mrs. Hatchfield assigned Ann the job of preparing all the meals again—for which her brothers were thankful.

The only task Mrs. Hatchfield did that they didn't was any shopping or errands, which Frank kept a log of, noting time of day, frequency, and duration.

Mrs. Hatchfield was abed and the kids were settling into their nightly "Operation Hatchetface" update in Tony, Benny, and Matty's room.

Benny launched right in.

"Okay, let's vote. I say we nuke her now," he proposed, raising his hand.

"We haven't even called the meeting to order yet, Benny," Frank pointed out as he updated his Hatchfield Charts tracking her behavioral patterns, activities, and schedule.

"Okay, I call this meeting to order," Benny amended.

"Second," Ann agreed.

"All those in favor of nuking Hatchetface, raise your hands," Benny proposed anew, lofting his.

"It's still too early," Frank argued.

Ann sniffed her hands, made a face, and raised one of them in solidarity with Benny.

Frank looked surprised.

"*Et tu*, Ann?"

"*Well*," Ann whined back, "I'm her 'kitchen slave,' and she buys weird food I then have to somehow make edible. I had to de-bone all the fish tonight and now I can't get the smell of it off my hands."

"And I smell too, thanks to her—like her *ashtray*," Benny piped in, "because she's decided I'm her ashtray-carrier—I have to follow her around from room to room with it! I might as well strap it to my head!"

Randy laughed.

"It's not funny! Today Missus Fowler was gonna send me to the principal's office for smoking! It took me all first recess to convince her it was stinky ol' Missus Hatchfield she was smelling!"

"Just hide from her," Tony suggested. "That's what I do. I don't even think she remembers how many of us there are. Anyway, I vote with Frank. I say we wait."

"She makes me empty her ashtrays and vacuum up

her butts," Randy added. "And she doesn't get any of my butt jokes. Like, when I told her I wasn't happy being her butt-sucker, she didn't even crack a smile."

Matty and Benny laughed.

"Thank you!" Randy responded with a nod of appreciation. "I think she had her sense of humor cut out at birth," he continued. "But it's probably too early to nuke her, I don't know... I guess... I abstain.

"Two for and two against, it's up to you Matty," Frank posed.

Matty wasn't sure how to vote. Spending his days with the nuns was not much different, annoyance-wise, than spending his afternoons with Missus Hatchfield. Still, she wouldn't ever give him a penny when he asked, even after several of his best super-cute efforts. She seemed immune to his powers. But now it had become a challenge—a challenge he wasn't quite yet ready to concede.

"Too early," he voted.

"There you have it," Frank nodded. "So for now, we continue to chart her weaknesses and play her victims."

Benny moaned.

Ann rolled her eyes, sniffed her fishy hands again, and made a face.

"Maybe if I wash them in tomato juice?"

The kids honored the vote and continued playing their roles as victims. They looked sufficiently cowed at her orders and mock-polite. Randy was the wild card, but Mrs. Hatchfield grasped neither his humor nor his sarcasm so, so far, they were still okay.

Ann returned home with Matty and parked the car in the driveway next to Mrs. Hatchfield's.

School was out for the Christmas break, which meant Matty didn't have to go back to St. Helena's, so they were both feeling pretty content. In another two weeks their Dad would return and they would all have Christmas together.

Ann had determined to make it the best Christmas possible.

She wasn't yet to the point of realizing that repeating what she just tried at Thanksgiving and expecting a different result was the definition of insanity. She had a whole preparation and decorating strategy to spring on her siblings and enlist their help so they could *all* surprise their dad when he got home, hoping to unite the family and put him in the Christmas spirit.

But... this time she would need all her brothers' help to pull it off.

Frank had been in a particularly good mood lately— thanks to him, via Miss Espy, the school administration had announced they were granting Billy Bobbs' family his high school diploma posthumously, so Ann figured Frank might be up for celebrating. Plus, usually where Frank went her other brothers would follow.

They entered the house and Ann went up to her room to stow her books and start thinking about anything but school.

Matty trotted off to the kitchen for a snack before searching out and seeing what interesting things his brothers might be up to. When he reached the kitchen, he was startled to find Mrs. Hatchfield standing over the sink, mumbling to herself.

Maybe he would try to hit her up for a penny again.

"Unbelievable..." she grumbled, "...foul, gross, disgusting, putrid, unsanitary thing."

Curious, Matty approached and extended the set of drawers to create his stairway up. As he did he heard a shaking noise and saw Mrs. Hatchfield was sifting salt into the sink.

Matty peered in to see poor Lugee fizzling, foaming, and turning green under a blanket of it.

"Die!" Mrs. Hatchfield insisted. *"Die!"*

Matty screamed.

Mrs. Hatchfield had ensconced herself in the master bedroom for the night and the Benjamin kids had reassembled in the boys' room for the nightly Hatchfield Chart update.

Matty, still red-faced from hours of crying, sat in Ann's lap with his head buried in her shoulder.

Randy's hand shot up first.

"Okay. All those in favor of massive retaliation, raise your hand," he proposed.

Benny raised both hands, Tony raised his and nodded, Ann's went up next, and Matty raised one without looking up. Everyone waited for Frank.

After pausing in contemplation and a final scan of his Hatchfield Charts, Frank slowly but determinedly raised his hand too.

"You all know the plan and have your assignments," Frank said, looking at each of his siblings. "Operation Hatchetface will be tomorrow. No mercy."

As anticipated in Frank's charts and like clockwork, following breakfast and cleanup, Mrs. Hatchfield drove off on her round of grocery shopping and errands.

From the upstairs window the Benjamin kids surreptitiously watched her car drive down the street, turn a corner and disappear.

Frank checked his watch.

"Go," he announced.

The kids immediately headed out in different directions.

Ann popped the latch on the master bedroom door and zeroed in on the closet where all of Mrs. Hatchfield's clothes were hung. She reached in her pocket to pull out her seam ripper, holding it up like a murder weapon as she removed Mrs. Hatchfield's bathrobe from the closet and turned it inside out on the bed to run the ripper smoothly and neatly along all the major inside seams. She very gently replaced the robe on its hanger and went for the next garment in line.

Randy pulled his junior chemistry set out from under his bed. He extracted a bottle labeled, "potassium nitrate" and one of his small beakers. He went to the bathroom to mix a saturated solution of the chemical and water.

Meanwhile, Benny and Matty had gathered Mrs. Hatchfield's chocolate boxes. They hid the unopened one under Tony's bed, then carefully removed and inserted a piece of Chocolate Ex-Lax into the underside of each chocolate from her already open box, before carefully placing them neatly back into their pleated paper pockets.

Tony busied himself in the master bathroom. He removed the roll of toilet paper from the holder, replacing it with an empty cardboard tube. He then took all the remaining rolls out from under the cupboard beneath the sink. He started to leave, but then returned to grab the box of tissues too.

Frank went down in his laundry room/workshop. He emptied Mrs. Hatchfield's bottle of home permanent solution down the sink and, using a funnel, refilled the bottle with Nair hair-remover lotion.

Randy and Frank's room became a factory assembly line: Randy painted each of Mrs. Hatchfield's cigarettes with potassium nitrate, Tony blew them dry with Ann's hair dryer, Benny and Matty carefully refilled the dry ones back into their boxes, and Frank joined them to reseal and restack the packs into their carton.

As Ann finished seam ripping the last of every piece of Mrs. Hatchfield's clothing she could find, being careful to place everything back exactly where she found it, Benny and Matty placed the tainted chocolate box on the bedside table exactly where they found it, Frank put the hair products back in the shower where he found them, and Tony and Randy put her carton and packs of cigarettes back where they found them.

After a quick scan of the room, everyone nodded.

Frank latched the master bedroom door and pulled it closed.

The kids were all in Matty, Benny, and Tony's room

gorging themselves on the untainted box of chocolates they had stolen from Mrs. Hatchfield's room when they heard her pull up and the car door slam.

They all dashed down to stop on the stairwell, giggling to themselves as they awaited her entry.

Mrs. Hatchfield hung her coat in the hall closet and looked up at them, scowling.

They looked back with deadpan faces.

"Eeeh... What's up, doc?' Randy asked.

Frank hit him.

"Don't just stand there," Mrs. Hatchfield commanded, "Get the groceries from the car and put them away." She pushed past them heading up the stairs to continue, "Then bring me some coffee and stay out of my hair."

"Yess'um," Frank replied, as they all headed out the door.

Ann hesitated. She heard the master bedroom door close. She crossed to the hall closet, grabbed Mrs. Hatchfield's coat, and, brandishing her seam ripper again, smiled.

Jeopardy was on the TV and Mrs. Hatchfield had her shoes off, was propped up on the bed by pillows, and on her third cigarette and sixth chocolate when there was a knock at her door.

"Come in," she croaked.

"It's me," Frank answered as he entered through the haze of smoke, "I brought your coffee."

"It's about time."

Frank set the cup on the bedside table and glanced at the already half-eaten box of doctored chocolates next to it.

169

He deliberately bumped her current pack of cigarettes onto the floor so he could palm the last remaining two before placing the empty pack back on the bedside table.

"Oops, sorry—no harm done," Frank explained before heading out.

"Lock the door after you when you leave," Mrs. Hatchfield ordered.

"With pleasure."

The door double-clicked shut.

Mrs. Hatchfield's tummy made a grumble. She took a few sips of coffee.

I'm just hungry.

So... she took *another* chocolate.

Her current cigarette was down to the filter tip—she snuffed it out and reached for the pack, shook it... but it was empty. The new carton was across the room on the dresser so she reluctantly heaved herself up to pop it open and get out a fresh pack. Once up, she figured she might as well take her shower and do her hair before *Search for Tomorrow* started, so she stripped, dropping her clothes in a pile by the bed, and crossed to the bathroom to turn on the shower.

After her shower, she put her hair up in curlers and blocked her face with cotton before using her permanent solution to coat and wrap her head.

Her gut gurgled uncomfortably.

She finished wrapping and went to her make-up bag, applying her foundation, rouge, and drawing on an eyebrow.

Her gut gurgled insistently, and lower down this time, causing her to stop at one eyebrow and lurch for the toilet bowl.

"Damn."

She opened her new pack of cigarettes and lit one as she sat.

The cigarette paper burned like a fuse, dumping tobacco all over her and the floor, leaving nothing but the filter tip in her mouth.

"What the...?"

She tried a second, with the same result. But before she could process this oddity, her gut let go.

Out in the hallway, Benny and Matty were listening at the door to the horrible, disgusting sounds coupled with Mrs. Hatchfield's groans.

"Eeew!" they nasaled to each other and then laughed, after a particularly repulsive sound emanated.

"Benny! Matty! Lunch is ready!" Ann called up from the kitchen.

"*Lunch...?*" Benny commented to Matty, scrunching his nose, as the boys headed down to the kitchen.

"Well...?" Ann asked, wanting an update.

"Definitely *indisposed,*" Benny laughed.

The sun was setting on the Benjamin house when Matty left his post at the master bedroom door and joined the others in the living room, where Frank, Randy, and Tony had built a huge maze out of every book in the shelves to run the rats though and time them with a stop watch.

"Fireworks are over," Matty announced.

"It's only intermission," Frank corrected, as he clicked the stopwatch when Chocolate-Drop reached the end of the maze and Randy fed the rat a raisin. "Chocolate-Drop was almost two full seconds faster that time."

Frank reset the stopwatch, nodded, and Tony dropped Mucklethorp into the middle of the maze as he started the watch again.

Her gut finally cleared, Mrs. Hatchfield breathed a sigh of relief, and was now solidly convinced.

Those brats are trying to kill me. They must have poisoned my coffee. Well, I'll show those little rodents they can't mess with Bea Hatchfield!

She reached for some toilet paper to wipe herself only to find an empty roll. She next leaned over to check under the sink for a spare roll—none to be found.

"ANN!" she screamed at the top of her voice. "ANN BENJAMIN, COME HERE THIS **INSTANT!**"

Ann dashed up the stairs to the master bedroom door.

"Yes, Missus Hatchfield?"

"BRING ME SOME TOILET PAPER, *NOW!*"

"No problem... be right back," Ann replied brightly while stomping her feet in place progressively more gently to mimic the sound of her running off, then doing the reverse to continue her charade by rattling the doorknob and calling back, "Mrs. Hatchfield? The door's locked. I can't get in."

Her brothers, who had gathered at the base of the stairs to enjoy Ann's performance, all could barely stifle their glee.

Matty added, in a sing-songy voice," Too bad."

Ann put a finger to her lips to shush them and quietly popped the latch on the door, returning seconds later with the clothes Mrs. Hatchfield had been wearing. She came down stairs and handed the clothing to Randy.

"Hide those somewhere."

Ann pulled a wad of bills out of her pocket too.

"I rescued what's left of the spending money Dad gave her from the envelope in her purse," she explained while they all eyed the pile of loot.

Mrs. Hatchfield stomped her feet in frustration. She dug though the trash to find something with which to wipe herself, extracting the list of instructions for her home permanent solution.

Matty, Benny, and Ann made Dagwood sandwiches for everyone, dealing out sliced meats, cheeses, and lettuce onto mayonnaise and mustard-slathered bread like they were dealing cards.

Tony added handfuls of potato chips to each plate.

Randy stood at the stove making Jiffy Pop.

Frank was on drink duty, pouring out glasses of milk for everyone.

"Shouldn't we make one for Mrs. Hatchfield?" Benny asked, with a grin.

"She won't be staying," Ann grinned back.

They all heard the toilet flush upstairs.

"Here comes the finale, guys," Frank announced, grabbing his glass of milk and a plate, heading for the living room. "Let's hurry. We'll wanna get good seats."

Frank hesitated, stopped everyone, and then returned to the phone, where he had set out his tape recorder.

"Hold up. I don't know *how* I could have forgotten *this* part," he confessed, blushing, as he dialed a number he had written on a piece of paper.

A man's voice on the other end answered, "Hello...?"

Frank hit "play" on his tape recorder and put the receiver's microphone up to the speaker.

"Harry," Mrs. Hatchfield's voice said," This is Bea

173

Hatchfield, and for the past eight years I've claimed *half* of what I earned, so what are you gonna do about it?!"

"What!" her boss, Harry, responded, following up with a rant full of expletives.

Frank, play-acting Mrs. Hatchfield, slammed down the receiver, rudely hanging up on him.

Mrs. Hatchfield stepped stiff-legged to the mirror. She had virtually forgotten about her hair until she had to wipe herself with the instructions—now panic had set in.

She carefully unwrapped her curlers and quickly worked to remove one of them.

The curler simply dropped off into her hand, hair and all.

"Oh—my—*God*..." she gasped. She barely touched another and it fell off into the sink, followed by several more, revealing her bald head beneath.

"NOOOOOOOO!!!"

Resembling a radiation victim, Mrs. Hatchfield finished rinsing her raw head, then burst from the bathroom into the master bedroom and crossed to the closet. She threw on her bathrobe only to have it fall apart at the seams and crumple to the floor in pieces. She saw the cup of coffee on the bedside table and crossed to look into it, panic-stricken. She had only had a few sips of it, but was now convinced she had been poisoned by it.

She clutched her stomach.

What did they give me? I need to get out of here. Get to a hospital! I can't spend one more minute in this hell house!

She opened the closet, extracted her suitcases, and quickly tossed all her clothes into them from both the closet and dresser.

She extracted a bra and panties and donned them only to have them burst apart at the seams too. She tried more clothes—all with the same result.

A bald and hysterical Mrs. Hatchfield bounded down the stairs toting her purse and suitcases, and wearing nothing but a large bath towel, her shoes, one eyebrow, and her silly hat hiding her bald head while the kids sat in a circle around the coffee table watching her and munching popcorn, as if they were viewing their favorite movie.

"Why, Mrs. Hatchfield!" Randy exclaimed with a mock-gasp and a hand to his chest, "You're not decent!"

She raised her suitcases in front of herself protectively.

They all stood and slowly approached her, grinning ominously.

"Stay back! All of you!" she growled.

"Your suitcases...?" Tony asked. "Are you *leaving* us?"

"Don't play dumb, you little monsters!"

She crossed to the hall closet to get her coat, and donning it, she shimmied out of the towel, closed the jacket's belt, and kicked the towel toward the kids.

"Here!" she said, "I don't want to *ever* set foot in this hell-house again!"

She dashed out the door to her car as the kids followed. She extracted her keys and bent over to unlock the door.

The back of her jacket split open at the seam, revealing her big, old naked butt.

"The end," Matty giggled.

The Benjamin kids all shared a well-earned laugh as Mrs. Hatchfield drove away.

"We're on our own now," Frank proclaimed.

"Hallelujah!" Randy sang out, raising his hands aloft.

They all felt triumphantly happy. Ann was the first to ponder what should happen next.

"I wonder if we should call Dad?" she questioned, feeling a twinge of guilt.

"Absolutely not!" Frank shot back, "Hatchetface won't dare call him—what could she even say? 'I mistreated and then abandoned your kids?' No—I'm sure we're good till he gets back. And I want to make the most of it."

We're *waaaay* better off without her," Tony insisted.

"We always take care of ourselves anyway," Benny reminded.

"And who's gonna know she's not here except us?" Randy added as they went back into the house.

Next door, Mrs. Coe had been observing Mrs. Hatchfield's dramatic exit from her kitchen window.

Chapter Nine

Murphy's Lawbreakers

The Benjamin kids finished the evening with celebratory ice cream cones when Ann announced, "I have something important to propose to you guys."

"Not marriage," snarked Randy.

"Don't be a toad," she replied. "No, this is about us, and Dad, about us as a *family*."

A collective groan rose from her brothers.

"No, *listen*! Hear me out! We have a little more than a week and a half before Dad gets back and then it's Christmas," Ann launched in, "and I have a plan but I'll need all you guys to help me if we're gonna pull it off."

She crossed to the fireplace hearth and turned to address the rest more formally, buoyed with enthusiasm.

"Look, we haven't had a really *good* family Christmas since... well, since before Momma died. And this'll probably be our last Christmas here at *home*. So I want to do it up **big**—the way we used to! For **Momma!** You know—get a big tree, put up all the decorations, bake lots of cookies together, and do up the house inside and out, and exchange gifts with each other...."

There was a lot of ice cream cone licking going on but no real reaction.

"...*Well*?" Ann prodded. "What do you guys think? You up for it?"

The other boys all glanced at Frank.

Sigh.

Ann knew the drill—if Frank was on board the others would more likely follow. She kicked herself for not trying to convince Frank alone first.

Frank got his ice cream licked down below the edge of the cone so he could pause to respond without dripping.

"I think the best Christmas gift we could all give each other is a week and a half of letting each other do whatever we want with our freedom. I mean, Dad's gone, Hatchetface is gone, we all have stuff we *want* to do—this may be our only time in a very long while for each of us to do whatever we want without *anyone* around to say no. For me, I'm only a day or two away from finishing my laser."

Randy nodded in agreement.

"I need to finish my movie, and you can star in it," he told Tony, nudging him.

Tony grinned, "Cool."

Ann saw she was losing them. Frank noticed Ann's disappointment.

"Look. *You* can still do up Christmas, Ann, if that's what *you* want to do, no one is stopping you," he offered. "That's my whole point."

"Let's vote," Randy insisted, cutting to the chase. "All those in favor of everyone doing whatever they want until Dad gets home, raise your hand."

Randy and Frank's hands went up immediately, followed by Tony's. Benny stared into his lap, still contemplating.

Matty finally raised his hand and shot Ann a sympathetic, "Sorry."

"Meeting adjourned," Randy piped.

"Second," Tony confirmed.

The three older boys and Matty went off to their rooms to pursue their own grand plans, leaving Ann and Benny alone.

Benny looked up.

"I wanna do Christmas with you," he decided. "Do you still wanna?"

Ann smiled and sat next to him. She could always count on Benny.

She pulled over her notepad she had on the coffee table where her plans were all written out. She picked up her pencil and started editing.

"With just the two of us we'll have to pare down some of this, but we can still have fun, huh? Bake Christmas cookies and decorate a tree together and stuff?"

"Yup."

Entropy expands quickly when it is multiplied by six. In less than 48 hours the Benjamin house was a disaster. A three-foot-long half-finished model of a rocket hung from a broomstick Randy had braced across the curtain rods in one corner of the living room. There were dirty dishes, pizza boxes, comic books, toys, playing cards, and kittens everywhere.

Even some dog poop no one had yet noticed or stepped in.

Ann had dragged all the dusty boxes of old Christmas decorations in from the garage and stacked them here and there in various rooms, while she had cookbooks splayed out on the coffee and kitchen tables from which to glean her holiday recipes.

Tony, who played the lead spaceman in Randy's movie, had made his own costume, so most of the kitchen table was a pile of silver stretch fabric next to the sewing machine, cans of silver spray paint, and a silver-painted and doctored football helmet that now resembled a space helmet.

Matty was simply content to sit under the kitchen table for hours on end with his construction paper and crayons and draw.

Benny counted his handful of change for the third time before shoving it into his pocket.

It should be enough.

"Frank?!" he hollered.

Hearing no response, Benny descended the stairs, which had become coated with various piles of things once intended to go up or down but other distractions now left neglected and in *everyone's* way.

"Ann?!" Benny yelled.

"What is it, Benny?' she answered as she rushed into the entryway and grabbed her coat from the closet.

"Will you walk with me to Woolworth's? I'm not allowed to go that far on my own."

"I can't right now, honey. I need to run to the grocery for a sec to get powdered ginger so we can make some gingerbread cookie dough after dinner. Frank?!!"

Frank didn't respond.

"Benny, could you tell Frank to take the casserole out of the oven when the buzzer rings?"

"But I need to go to Woolworth's!"

"And if he won't, get someone else to do it—I'll be right back."

Ann dashed out to the car.

Benny wandered into the kitchen to find Matty lying on his back under the table, staring at its underside again.

He continued on into the laundry room where Frank was deep into the first tests of his working laser.

A brilliant red beam bounced around between several mirrors. The last mirror shot the beam across the room where it hit the wall. The wall began to smoke.

Benny noticed several other burn marks there already.

"Shoot."

Frank clicked it off and re-aimed the mirrors.

"Frank?"

"Not now, Benny."

"Ann asked me to ask *you*..."

"***Not now**, Benny!*"

Benny continued on into the dark garage where Randy lay on his back, camera secured to a tripod and aimed at the ceiling.

Randy and Tony had draped tar paper across the ceiling, poked holes in it, and set a light behind it to create a field of stars.

Tony was costumed in his space suit and helmet, and suspended from the ceiling, as were both of the rats.

Looking up through Randy's viewfinder, Tony and the rats appeared to be slowly floating and spinning through space—until Benny's head popped into the frame at an odd angle, ruining the shot.

"Benny!" Randy growled, stopping his camera, "Get out of my shot!"

"But I need someone to walk me to Woolworth's. And Ann wants one of you guys to watch dinner," Benny added.

"Just spin the rats and get out of my shot!" Randy yelled.

Benny gently tapped each rat, setting them spinning

181

again. Mucklethorp squeaked his displeasure with the situation, and Tony was right there with him.

"How much longer will this take?" Tony gasped. "The lights are hot and I can barely breathe in this harness."

"Okay, great, perfect! Go with it—act like you are running out of air!" Randy decided. "*Killer Rats from Outer Space* will soon invade the world."

Suddenly there was a pop-flash through the window in the laundry room door and the power went out, plunging the garage into total darkness and blowing one of Randy's bulbs.

"Great!" Randy fumed, stomping toward the laundry room and bumping Tony in the process, setting him spinning out of control.

"Dammit! Get me down from here!"

Randy burst into the laundry room.

"Frank, you just ruined my shot!" he fumed.

"Sorry, the fuse blew when I upped the power—I'll fix it."

Frank and Randy dashed off to the main fuse box leaving Benny alone in the laundry room and Tony still spinning and yelling vainly for help.

But then it dawned on Benny—this was *his* week to do whatever *he* wanted to too. Right? Everyone else was breaking the rules. Doing whatever *they* wanted. And he knew the way to Woolworth's and back. He could do it all on his own.

Matty saw the lights come back on and heard the oven fire up again.

From his vantage point on the floor, lying on his back and staring straight up at it, the door his dad had turned into a kitchen table looked like a door floating in midair.

A magic door.

Matty had drawn a doorknob onto its underside with crayon.

The oven timer buzzed. Matty ignored it—and no one else was in earshot to hear it.

Matty still wasn't sure where his magic door might lead. Somewhere more interesting than here in their house, no doubt. Maybe a jungle? Or a different planet? Or inside a huge stone castle... on a tropical island?

It could really lead anywhere.

Or maybe it could take him to different places *each time* he opened it?

Matty reached for the knob. With his back glued to the floor by gravity, he couldn't reach it to turn it. Not even close. He was still way too small.

It might be years before he would be big enough to actually reach, to go somewhere other than here, to see what was out there, he figured. So for now, as a little kid, all he could do was stay here and imagine.

He had also drawn a keyhole under the knob, but he hadn't yet drawn a key for it.

Maybe I'll do that next.

As he stared at the door, lost in thought, the room around his magic door began to slowly fade and the door seemed to be floating off into the clouds. The clouds darkened into storm clouds, soon billowing around it, darker and darker... **smoke?!**

"**FIRE!**" Matty screamed, scrambling out from under the table to find the kitchen full of black smoke and flames licking from the oven door to the cabinets over the stovetop, catching them afire.

"**FIRE! HELP!** *FIRE!*"

Matty was still screaming and the oven still buzzing when Frank, Randy, and Tony burst in, followed by Ann, arriving back from the store. Frank dashed over to open the sliding glass door and raced back to the fuse box again to snap off the oven's breaker while Randy and Tony threw glasses and pans full of water on the various flames until they were all out.

Frank opened more windows. The air began to clear.

The phone rang.

The kids all stood and stared at the horrible swath of charred kitchen before them, struck dumb.

Ann finally snapped out of her stupor and picked up Matty to console him.

She turned to Frank, glaring.

"Dammit! I told you guys to watch dinner!" she snapped, setting Matty back down.

"You *never* told me to watch dinner!"

"Yes I *did*, I specifically told *Benny* to tell *one of you* to watch dinner!"

"The phone's ringing," Matty interjected.

"He never told me!"

"Me neither," Randy added.

"I was tied up so none of this is my fault!" Tony remarked from inside his space helmet.

"The phone's ringing!" Matty interjected again, more loudly.

"BENNY!!!" Ann, Frank, Randy, and Tony all hollered, but there was no answer.

"Where's *is* Benny?" Ann wondered.

"He's in the hospital," Matty answered, handing Ann the phone receiver.

The Benjamin kids sat in the hospital's emergency waiting room. An ambulance siren quieted itself before pulling up to admit a new patient.

Hearing the siren, Matty knit his brows and tugged on Ann's sleeve, worried.

"Is Benny gonna die too?" he asked.

Ann put her arms around Matty and pulled him close in a hug while trying not to cry herself.

Frank stared at the floor, lost in guilty thoughts.

Randy paced while having an unhappy internal conversation with himself.

Tony wiped his eyes on his shirtsleeve, hoping the other kids didn't see him crying.

Finally their family doctor, Dr. Vance, pushed a wheelchair with a bruised and banged-up Benny through the doors into the waiting room. Benny had a cast on one leg and a pair of crutches held diagonally across his lap.

"Here's your brother," Dr. Vance said, smiling. "I wish I could say as good as new. It looks worse than it is. He's actually a very lucky young man. Most people who pick fights with cars don't get up again."

"Doctor Vance, thank you for coming to the hospital to check on him," Ann sighed.

185

Dr. Vance turned to Ann and Frank.

"The hospital alerted me right away. Hit and run," he said, shaking his head. "I don't understand how someone could *do* that."

The kids all gathered around Benny with looks of relief while Benny only glanced back at them, embarrassed and glum.

"I'm okay," Benny mumbled.

"Too bad you lived, junior," Randy smirked, "'cause Dad's gonna kill you."

"I tried to get ahold of your father," Dr. Vance explained, "but there was no answer at the number I had. I'll try again when I get back home."

"*No!*" all the kids spontaneously blurted.

"It's okay, we'll call him when we get home," Frank covered. "Actually... our sitter, Missus Hatchfield, she's at home right now trying to reach him. She's probably already talked to him."

"Being responsible for us and all, I'm sure she'd prefer the news comes from her, you understand," Ann added.

"I see," Dr. Vance answered. "Well, let him and your sitter know that if either of them has any questions at all, they can call me anytime. Benny's cast should come off in about three weeks."

The doctor glanced around at the kids.

"I'm a little surprised your sitter isn't here with you."

"She thought it best to stay by the phone, in case Dad called there," Tony vamped.

Ann tried to change the subject, asking, "Um, are there any papers we should sign or anything...?"

"Nope, I took care of all that—I'm glad I had your father sign medical releases for each of you kids before he left town."

"I'll say," Randy mumbled under his breath.

Tony and Frank nudged him quiet.

Ann went around the back of the wheelchair and started Benny for the door, thinking it best they limit any further conversation with Dr. Vance. They all gave more cheery 'thank-you's to him as Tony and Randy jumped on the automatic door opener and Ann wheeled Benny out to the station wagon to lay him out flat in the rear of it while Frank ran the chair back into the hospital so they could *get-the-heck home.*

The Benjamin kids all sat around in the charred and smoke-stained kitchen, just staring at it. The oven and stove top were toast, as were the cupboards above. The paint on the ceiling right above the stove had bubbled to bits and the rest of the ceiling was coated in black soot.

The nearby curtains were brown and crispy from the heat.

Randy went over and pried open the oven door, extracting a slightly melted casserole dish full of charcoal.

"Even *I* can't eat this."

"Dad's gonna kill me," Ann whimpered. "He's gonna say this is all my fault."

"It's not your fault," Matty consoled her.

"It's Benny's," Randy decided.

"Is *not!*" Benny moaned from his kitchen chair.

Ann crossed and sat at the table next to Benny and put her hands on his shoulders, consoling him.

The other kids joined them around the table.

Take care of your dad and brothers.

Ann heard her mother's words. Try as she might, she was unable to fulfill the request.

She had failed.

A tear rolled down her cheek.

She wiped it away.

"It's not your fault, Benny," Ann sighed, admitting defeat. "It's *mine*. I can't take care of you guys and Dad. It's no use."

She shot a look of dread at Frank.

"C'mon, Frank. We need to go call Dad and tell him the whole ugly truth."

Frank, who had remained in quiet contemplation, got up with her and followed her to the phone, but when Ann reached for it, he took the receiver from her and hung it back up.

"Wait," he said, raising a finger.

He looked Ann in the eyes then glanced at the others.

"Wait just a *second*..."

Frank lit up in a grin and addressed his siblings.

"Before we do something... rash, let's think about this for a minute," he orated, pointing at the stove. "So, okay... the oven is a bit... *crispy*. So we have no adult supervision, the house is a *total* mess, and Benny looks like hamburger meat. But, answer me *this*:"

He crossed to Tony, pointing to him proudly.

"Who was clever enough to get his substitute teacher to *blow up* his classroom, *eh*?"

Tony chuckled.

Frank turned to Matty.

"Who mastered the fine art of Bugs Bunny and successfully *shot the moon*?"

Matty smiled.

He pointed to Randy.

"Who got Hatchetface to *quit smoking*?"

Randy laughed.

He crossed to place his hands on Benny's shoulders.

"Who, although he now resembles hamburger meat himself, was able to *single-handedly* turn Bosco into hamburger meat?"

Benny smiled wanly for the first time all evening.

Frank stood in front of the group and gestured to himself in mock-humility.

"Who got Jefferson High to *graduate a dead person*?"

Frank offered a hand to Ann and pulled her up next to him, presenting her to the rest of the family.

"And... who designed Missus Hatchfield a *whole new daring wardrobe*?"

Ann blushed out a grin and mock-curtsied, as her brothers all applauded her.

Frank turned to Ann, facing her eye to eye, with a more serious look.

"What about it, Annie. Answer me one question: ***What would Momma think?***"

Ann felt a chill; she could almost sense the presence of their mother in the kitchen with them at that very moment, waiting, like all her brothers were, to hear her answer too.

Sure—she had asked Ann to take care of all of them, but what *exactly* did she mean by that? Their mother only ever saw the good in each one of them. She constantly reminded each of them of their innate talents—she lauded and trusted in those talents. Encouraged all of them to rely on their curiosity, creativity, and craft—and to lean on *each other*.

189

Maybe that's what she meant? For *Ann* to continue *believing* in all of them too? The way *she* always had?

"She'd think... we *can* handle this... but only *if* we all work **together**," Ann proclaimed.

The phone rang—everyone froze.

Ann gulped, crossed to it, and answered.

"Hello...?"

She cringed, swallowed again, and put on her perkiest voice, "Oh hi, Daddy! How *are* you? How's the project going? Fine! Oh, yeah, we're all *great*! We were just... straightening up the kitchen before we get ready for bed.

"Missus Hatchfield? No, um... she can't come to the phone just now. She... ran out for a sec. I think she needed something... for her hair."

Randy snickered. Ann shushed him and grabbed for the pad and a pencil.

"But how are *you*, Daddy? Is work going okay? When do you think you'll be able to come home? Like what day—*exactly*? What time is your flight...? Really?! Not till Christmas Eve?! *Good!*

"I mean I'm glad you'll be home for Christmas! Um-hum. Everything's *fine*. Nope. Nothing unusual. Missus Hatchfield...? Well, to be honest, Daddy, we didn't like her at first, but we... well, we all came to an understanding. I think she *reeeally* gets us now and so... it's like... like she's not even here.

"Everyone else is fine, they all say 'hi'," Ann offered as she gestured to the boys to respond.

"Hi! Hi Dad!" they all hollered cheerily.

The doorbell rang. Everyone froze again.

"I have to go, Daddy—someone's at the door. Okay—I

will. *I will!* Bye, Dad—bu-bye!"

She hung up, letting out a huge sigh of relief.

"Saved by the bell."

Not necessarily," Randy replied after peering through the front door peep hole and seeing Mrs. Coe's fish-eyed face through the lens.

Frank peeked next, then put the chain on the door.

"Let me take this one," he told the rest of them, "and whatever happens follow my lead."

Frank opened the door a crack—only what the chain would allow.

"Oh, Hello, Missus Coe," he said, greeting her through the crack.

Mrs. Coe tried in vain to see in, but couldn't, so she huffed and replied, "I'd like to speak with your babysitter, please. I haven't seen her the past few days and her car hasn't been around. Is she here?"

"She's... *ouch!* Stop that! Her car is in for repairs," Frank stomped his foot, pretending to chase something away. "Sorry... Mrs. Hatchfield's upstairs. She's *indisposed* at the moment. That's how she likes us to say it. But you can come in and wait until she's done... *indisposing*. That is... if you don't mind wild rats."

Randy took Frank's cue, nodded, and dashed off.

"Rats...?" Mrs. Coe questioned.

Frank sighed and shook his head.

"My brother Randy's pet rats got loose again. He has dozens of them. And ever since he's been feeding them raw hamburger meat they've taken to *biting* people. It's quite annoying, to be honest."

Frank closed the door, removed the chain, and opened it wide to face Mrs. Coe.

191

"Come on in. If they go for your ankles just kick at them—they'll eventually back off."

Mrs. Coe took a step back, but then gave Frank the once-over, got a look at the super-messy house, and decided to call his bluff.

"All right," she said as she approached the threshold, "I *will* come in and wait."

Just as she crossed the threshold Randy entered holding a squeaking Chocolate-Drop out in front of himself, like the rat was a bomb about to go off, and waved him toward Mrs. Coe.

"Hah! Look out! *Got* one of the little buggers!"

The other kids squealed and backed away in mock-fear of the rat.

Mrs. Coe recoiled back to the porch and turned to make a hasty retreat, threatening, as she vanished into the dark of the night, "I'll be back tomorrow!"

Matty switched to the top bunk to give Benny the lower. Frank lifted Benny into his bed and Ann pulled up his covers. Frank set a walkie-talkie next to him.

"If you need to get up during the night call me," Frank instructed.

"I can get to the bathroom by myself."

"Like you got to Woolworth's by yourself?" Frank mocked.

"Shut up."

Frank snatched back the walkie-talkie, started to leave, then reconsidered, and left the walkie-talkie for Benny anyway before departing.

Ann sat with Benny. Matty and Tony had already

fallen fast asleep.

"You gonna be okay?" Ann asked in a whisper.

"Fine," Benny sighed back.

Ann put a hand on his shoulder to comfort him and asked, "Benny? Why *did* you go off to the store on your own?"

He huffed.

"You can tell me. I won't be mad. Please, I want to know why you did it."

Benny remained tight-lipped and angry for a minute, thinking. He finally relented and pointed to his jacket.

"In my pocket."

Ann reached over and took his jacket off the floor next to his bed and unzipped one of the front pockets, extracting a small paper bag. She looked in the bag and pulled out a faux-leather key case, puzzled.

"It's for Dad. For Christmas," Benny confessed.

Ann looked at the key case with new eyes and held it more tenderly, like a treasured jewel. She carefully returned it to the bag and set the bag on his bedside table next to the walkie-talkie and smiled at Benny.

"We'll wrap it for him tomorrow. Dad's pretty lucky to have a kid like you."

"Sez you."

Ann got up, crossed to the door, and turned out the light.

"Sez me."

Chapter Ten

Group Rehab

The next morning the Benjamin kids got an early start on cleaning up their disaster-area of a house, each starting upstairs in their own bedrooms. Worst off was the master bedroom, still reeking from the foul combination of flatus, stale Marlboros, cheap perfume, and old age.

Randy and Frank bravely volunteered for the mission. Wearing bandanas splashed with vanilla across their faces to ward off the stink, they marched resolutely into the malodorous mess armed with mops, brushes, air freshener, buckets, and bleach. First order of business: open wide every window, then take down curtains for washing, and scrub out the bathroom.

After finishing their room upstairs, Tony and Benny attacked the living room and removed Randy's rocket model to store it in the garage.

Meanwhile Matty and Ann teamed up to give all their pets baths before cleaning the bathrooms.

They figured it would take a few more rounds of cleaning to get the whole house really looking good, but at least they had put a big dent in the worst of it.

Opening all the windows in the house and a light, cool breeze helped.

Basic cleanup completed, the family gathered as a group at ground zero: the kitchen.

Randy stood high on a ladder with a bucket of soapy water, washing soot off of the ceiling while Benny, Matty, and Tony washed cupboards, counters, and the floor around the stove, and Ann removed the browned and heat-crumbled

195

curtains.

Frank pulled his torso out of the oven, holding a cracked and blackened heating element.

"Toast!" he announced. "Well, have to replace the whole thing."

"And we're gonna *have* to paint the ceiling, this is *not* coming off," Randy added.

"At least three of the cabinets are wrecked too," Tony added.

"Plus the drapes are ruined," Ann added.

Ann went to the kitchen table with a pad of paper and pencil, jotting it all down. An old cigar box full of money they had amassed from each of their personal allowance savings—including Tony emptying his magic wallet into it—and various other sources, like scrounging though all the couch cushions and car seats—sat in front of her. She did a quick count and jotted that down too.

She stopped writing, swept an errant lock of hair back out of her face, tucked it behind an ear, and sighed.

"We have ninety-three dollars and sixty-seven cents in what we gathered up."

"Cool, that's a lot more than I figured," Randy responded, feeling encouraged.

"I made some calls earlier and did some checking around in the store ads. Replacing this model of our stove will cost somewhere between two hundred sixty to two hundred eighty dollars," she informed.

"Ai-chihuahua!" Tony gasped.

"And I found someone who can fix the cabinets— Lynn's cousin's a carpenter. After talking with him about the cost of the cabinet repairs, I'm guessing it'll be at *least* another hundred? I can make the drapes myself so we only need to pay for the fabric—that will save some money. And we can do *all* the painting ourselves.

"There's eighty seven twenty left in the grocery fund. If we only eat what's currently in the cupboards and the fridge till Dad gets back—which I *think* we can do—then we are still short..."

She checked her addition of their cash plus the grocery fund.

"...somewhere around two hundred seventy dollars-*ish*... more or less?"

The room went into a stunned silence for a few minutes.

Ann held up an envelope.

"There's the fifty bucks Dad left in an emergency fund, but if we touch that, he'll kill us."

"*This* isn't an emergency?" Randy asked pointedly, eyes agog.

"And he's gonna kill us either way," Tony added.

"Some of us are dead already," Benny groused.

"Look, we *have* to replace the stove, fix the cabinets, and repaint the kitchen, with or without Dad's help," Frank argued. :"Randy's right, this is an emergency. The fund goes in."

Ann opened the envelope and dropped the fifty dollars into the cigar box.

"How are we *still* gonna raise over two hundred dollars *and* get all this done before Dad gets home?" Ann asked, already feeling defeated.

"I have some ideas," Frank answered. "We'll do some more brainstorming... and I worked out a basic schedule last night. If we all do our part, we'll be fine."

The doorbell rang.

Frank turned to Ann and Randy.

"Okay. There she is—you know what to do."

Mrs. Coe rang again. Ann answered with a perky, "Good morning, Mrs. Coe, please come in."

Mrs. Coe stepped cautiously into the house, especially eying the floor.

"Oh, don't worry—we caught all the rats."

"Is your sitter available now? I wish to speak with her."

Mrs. Coe scanned the living room and entryway, which seemed surprisingly tidier than it looked the night before, but she sniffed the air and made a face, still smelling residual smoke.

"Just between you and me," Ann confided in a whisper," Mrs. Hatchfield isn't a very good housekeeper, *or cook*, and she smokes like a *chimney*. Terrible habit."

Mrs. Coe ignored Ann, took a few more steps into the living room, and looked up the stairwell, then called out, "*Ahem... Mrs. Hatchfield...?!*"

"I'm Bea Hatchfield!" Mrs. Hatchfield's voice answered from the kitchen.

Frank, dressed in the last of Mrs. Hatchfield's clothes Ann had stolen off the floor and Randy had hidden away, a lot of padding, and a Halloween wig done up in curlers and a hair net, quickly waddled from the kitchen into the downstairs bathroom, latching the door shut.

"Huh... she's *indisposed* again, I guess," Ann said, shrugging.

Mrs. Coe crossed from the living room to the bathroom door on the other side of the entry.

Horrible fart noises emanated.

"She does that a *lot*," Ann whispered, making a

disgusted face.

Inside the bathroom, Randy, who had been waiting there all along, made another nasty, wet fart noise using his mouth on the crotch of his arm while Frank had his tape recorder along with his list of all the footage numbers for each of Mrs. Hatchfield's comments at the ready.

Mrs. Coe tapped her foot impatiently and checked her watch.

"Would you like some tea or something while you wait?" Ann offered, adding in a confiding whisper, "*She may be a while...*"

"Maybe I could just talk to her through the door?" Mrs. Coe grumbled.

"That's what we usually do," Ann replied sympathetically, rolling her eyes.

Randy added a grunt to the front of his next big fart sound—them smothered a laugh at his own exquisite grossness.

Mrs. Coe edged toward the door and rapped her knuckles on it briskly anyway.

"Missus Hatchfield? It's Joy Coe from next door. I want to talk to you about these Benjamin children. I'm very concerned about the goings-on over here, and well... I want to make sure they are being properly supervised in their father's absence!"

Frank hit play and Mrs. Hatchfield's voice replied, "I keep 'em scared. Works every time."

Randy followed with a series of short farts and an,

"Aaaah...!"

"She quite honestly scares the poo out of me," Ann asided to Mrs. Coe, wide-eyed.

"Frankly, you need to take a firmer hand with them!" Mrs. Coe hollered back through the door. "I've talked with some of the other neighbors, and they agree with me. And I've had enough of them beating up my boy, giant arrows over my back fence, and flaming feces on my doorstep! I know these kids are behind it!"

"So what are you gonna do about it?!" Mrs. Hatchfield's voice challenged.

Mrs. Coe huffed. "If I have any more trouble, I'll go straight to the **authorities!**"

She turned from the bathroom door to address Ann with a scolding finger-wag.

"Straight to the authorities, young lady—you tell all your brothers and your father **that!**"

Mrs. Coe exited, slamming the door behind her. Benny, Matty, and Tony popped out from around the corner and Frank and Randy burst out of the bathroom to join the others.

Randy made one more *huge* fart noise and they all burst out laughing.

Frank slipped out of his costume.

Ann stopped laughing first and grew serious.

"You don't think she'll really *do* anything do you?"

"Nah," Frank countered, waving the thought off, "She's just a blow-hard. And anyway, right now we have something much more serious to focus on: Money."

"Money," Benny pondered.

"Money," Tony contemplated.

"Money!" Randy exclaimed.

"Money," Ann fretted.

"Money?" Matty asked.

"Back to the kitchen," Frank coaxed, "and we'll go over our plan."

First up was creating a bar graph to fill in as they amassed more money, which they pinned on the kitchen bulletin board over the top of their chore list.

As Frank put it, "Money is the new chore and three days is our window to fill this all in, so we'll then have enough time to spend it and still get everything done in time."

And next to the money bar graph was their new "To Do" list of all the repairs, purchases, cleaning, and painting with each kid assigned to those various tasks.

Ann dropped off Benny and Matty in front of Woolworth's with their large cardboard box full of every last kitten they could round up. Ann had helped them tie Christmas ribbons around each of their necks, making them adorably irresistible. Benny and Matty were almost as adorably irresistible, costumed like contemporary versions of Victorian paupers in their most ragamuffin clothes. Benny had fashioned a hand-made crutch to go with his cast, and both had mussed their hair and added some of the kitchen soot to their faces in order to look as pathetic as possible.

And Matty had painted a large cardboard sign, "Christmas Kitties--50¢ each."

"*Please* try to get rid of them *all*," Ann begged. "And I'll be back to pick you up in a couple of hours."

The boys weren't at a loss for customers—Christmas shopping was in full swing, and who could resist a fluffy kitten? The bulk of them went fast but last two runty ones were proving to be the most difficult to sell.

Benny trailed on his crutch with an ash gray kitten clinging to his shoulders after one younger woman who had talked herself out of buying it. He stumbled on purpose, and then mock-cried. The woman helped him back to their box and then, feeling sufficiently guilty, relented, buying the cute, puny thing.

Meanwhile, Matty followed a businessman with his last black kitten, holding it up to him, and pouring on the little angel-face routine. The guy wasn't buying, but Matty was able to at least talk him out of a penny anyway.

An elderly woman finally bought it for her grandkids.

With all the kittens finally gone, the boys returned to sitting and waiting for Ann by their box. They decided to have a contest to see which of them could make the most pathetic face, which led to a number shoppers tossing their spare change into their box as they left the store out of pity for them.

Ann entered the Home Economics room at Jefferson High and donned her apron, taking one of the open cooking stations.

Three other girls were already in position as Ann's friend, Lynn, dashed in and took the last empty station right next to hers.

The girls exchanged looks of nervous excitement and crossed their fingers.

Miss Haines stood at the front of the room with a

stylishly dressed, statuesque woman.

"Okay girls, we are ready to start," Miss Haines announced, clapping her hands to silence the anxious girls. "This is Missus Colbert, the food editor from Better Homes and Gardens Magazine—she represents the Future Homemakers of America contest and will be overseeing and judging your work today."

Miss Haines gestured to Mrs. Colbert.

"Thank you, Miss Haines," Mrs. Colbert replied, turning to the class. "Ladies, we at Better Homes and Gardens want to see your ingenuity and creativity in the kitchen," Mrs. Colbert explained. "Each of you has a fully-stocked cupboard, fully-stocked refrigerator, and a Better Homes and Gardens cookbook at the ready. Your assignment today is—prepare and present a full meal for six in the next two hours. It is up to you to set your own menu and make sure all your items are ready to eat at the same time. Ready..."

Miss Haines stood next to a large timer clock on the table at the front, hand on the button.

"...Aaaaaaaaand... *GO!*" Mrs. Colbert finished.

Ann grinned from ear to ear. She couldn't believe her dumb luck. *Were they kidding?* She could throw together a meal for six with her eyes closed. And she simply *had* to win that fifty bucks. She scanned her cupboard and fridge, crossed to her cookbook, and jotted down a menu plan in mere moments, while setting her oven temperature and placing several pots on her stove before any of the other girls had even finished assessing their foodstuffs.

Ann flew through the process like it was a lovely dance. She tied up a pork loin in rosemary sprigs, covered it, and set it in the hot oven to roast. Next she made a quick lard pie crust and, using a can of cherry filling she found in her cupboard, added a little lemon zest to it and a latticed top crust to pop that into the oven too. Meanwhile she mashed together boiled potatoes and carrots and made a creamy pork gravy to go with it from her loin drippings. Once the pie was egg washed to give the crust a nice shine and out to cool, she opened the pork roast pan, glazed it with some slightly thinned mint jelly, and raised the oven temp higher to brown and crust the top of it. She cleaned, peeled, and diced mixed vegetables, steamed them to just fork-tender, and tossed them with caramelized onions, melted butter, and a light dusting of paprika and a an even lighter hint of cumin before placing them next to her crispy on the outside-tender and juicy on the inside sliced medallions of pork and the mashed potatoes and carrots, and gravy, on a table set so tidily Emily Post herself couldn't have done it better.

By the time Ann lit the candles adorning her table, removed her apron, and raised her hand to indicate her meal was ready for judging with ten full minutes to spare, smoke was escaping one of the other girl's ovens and half of Lynn's steamed peas missed her bowl to roll across her preparation counter and onto the floor.

"This is the best pork loin I've *ever* tasted," Mrs. Colbert marveled. "It is cooked to perfection! And what made you think to use mint jelly as a glaze?"

"My Mom used to make it that way—would you like to try my dessert?" Ann asked, adding a generous scoop of vanilla ice cream alongside a wedge of still-warm cherry pie.

"Let *me* try," Miss Haines offered, eagerly intercepting the pie.

Ann left with a large bronze replica of a measuring cup, a promise of her photo appearing in the January issue of *Better Homes and Gardens*, qualification for the finals, and *a crisp fifty dollar bill*. She and the rest of the girls also got to keep the meals they created and as much of the leftover food in their refrigerators and cupboards as they could tote to their cars—Miss Haines explained that *Better Homes and Gardens* had supplied all the food and it would only go bad over the holidays if they didn't take it with them.

Lynn gave *all* of hers to Ann, and a couple of the other girls didn't want much of their stuff either, so Ann scored three chickens, a second pork loin, almost four dozen eggs, several pounds of hamburger, butter, and lard, a couple large boxes full of various canned goods, boxes of frozen veggies, bags and bags of sugar and flour, sacks of potatoes and onions, lots of dry pasta, and one large canned ham.

Ann picked up Matty and Benny and they all hurried home to put the groceries away. They now had more than enough food to last until their father's return, and Ann thought she could use the ham for Christmas Eve dinner when their Dad got back.

With Ann's fifty dollar bill and another five-fifty-six from kitten sales and beggar's alms, they were able to color in a sizeable swath on the bar chart.

While the kittens were being peddled and Ann was play-acting future-housewife, Tony went door to door offering to wash neighborhood cars. Tony's smile, good looks, and eager to please sales pitch were able to charm even the most resistant of them—and many of their neighbors' young daughters enjoyed watching him clean. Several two-car households wanted both of their cars washed, which doubled his money and was quicker for him to accomplish than just one at a time.

Before his hands had completely shriveled to prunes from the suds, at a dollar a car and a few generous tips, he went home after his long day to add another nine seventy five to the cigar box and chart.

Frank and Randy spent their entire day at the Chestnut Retirement Village dressed in silly Santa hats and offering to help the elderly residents there by hanging their Christmas lights, setting up their trees, and doing various holiday chores for them. The residents loved it and were more than generous—between the two of them the boys were able to amass a whopping forty-seven fifty and a feeling of real accomplishment when the whole village started lighting up just as they jumped back on their bicycles to head home.

Without a working oven they had to have Ann's leftover pork loin cold, but no one minded and Frank brought in a Coleman stove so they could rewarm her mashed potatoes and gravy. Tony commented that it was like being on a campout, so in that spirit Ann set out a tablecloth on the living room floor, and they ate off of paper plates. Frank made a fire in the fireplace, and they turned out all the lights, ate by candlelight and used flashlights, made s'mores for dessert, and told creepy stories to scare each other.

The next morning, after breakfast and cleaning up the dishes they had ignored from their campout the night before, the kids gathered around the kitchen table to assess their progress. As much of a dent as they put in their goal graph, they were *still* about one hundred and twenty bucks shy of their goal.

"At least we have enough now so we can buy the stove today," Ann sighed, "but we'll need to do something bigger if we want to make enough money to pay the carpenter and put everything else back to normal."

Ann looked like she was going to cry again. Matty came over and gave her a hug.

"I have some pennies saved up," Matty offered.

"A handful of pennies isn't gonna help us much, Matty," Randy smirked.

"My hidden treasure is bigger than that!" Matty defended.

"Yeah, enough to buy some bubble gum," Randy rubbed it in.

"More than *that*!" Matty shouted and launched himself, fists flying at his brother.

Frank, Tony, and Benny, excited by the brouhaha, cheered the fight on, but Ann would have none of it.

"*Stop it*, you two!" she shouted, wresting the scrabbling Matty away from Randy, who was preparing to drop-kick him.

Ann turned to Frank. "Frank! C'mon! This is *serious*. We can't be fighting with each other right now."

Frank snapped out of it and pulled Randy back.

"Leave Matty alone, Randy. He's just a kid."

Ann addressed a still squirming Matty, "It's okay, honey. We could *use* your pennies. *Anything* will help. Will you show me?"

Matty took Ann's hand and they headed out. The other brothers followed.

On their way up the stairs Benny wondered aloud, "What *did* happen to all those pennies he's always askin' people for?"

Matty led them all to the upstairs bathroom. He removed the bottom drawer on one side of the built-in vanity. The space beneath it was a full three inches deep in not only pennies, but lots of other change as well. Even a few bills!

"Holy smokes!" Tony laughed.

"There must be at *least* fifty dollars-worth of change

in here!" Frank guesstimated.

"Whoa, Matty," Randy apologized, "I'm sorry, bud. You're a human slot-machine!"

Everyone patted Matty on the back and Randy ran to get a couple of buckets and the spade from the garage so he could help Matty scoop it all out to count and roll later.

Ann called the carpenter who agreed to meet with her at the house later that afternoon, then the whole family climbed into the station wagon to go shopping for a new oven and range.

Sears had the exact same color and model of their current oven and range, and on sale too, but Ann became smitten with the new state of the art Frigidaire "Flair" range and oven combination—there were two elegant glass-fronted ovens above a slick range top that pulled out like a drawer.

It was sleek, modern, and *very cool*.

The other kids liked it too. But it was seventy-five dollars over budget—a budget they had yet to actually fully achieve.

Frank marveled at the engineering on the sliding range top and Ann contemplated the ease of cooking with a second oven.

Matty liked the pale blue color, even though it didn't match anything else in their current kitchen.

Randy grabbed one of the brochures and began reading aloud:

"A revolutionary new design in electric ranges to glorify your kitchen without built-in expense! Combines twin, glass-fronted ovens and a new, slide-in cooktop in one cabinet. No carpentering, no plastering, no additional wiring when replacing an electric range. No tearing-up your kitchen. Incredible? It's true!"

"We can't afford it," Ann sighed. "Besides, what would Dad say when he saw it?"

"Well... he won't be able to deny it has *flair*—it says so right here," Randy chuckled, pointing to the brochure.

"Um... Dad's gonna notice we have a new stove either way, no?" Tony pointed out.

"Let me try again," Randy offered. "We're in so much trouble already, *who cares!*"

They all laughed.

"But... seventy-five more dollars?" Frank pondered.

"We should get it anyway," Benny determined. "We can't just prove to Dad we're good. We have to prove to him we're *better* than all the other kids. We *have* to make the kitchen *better* than it was. We have to make *everything* better than it was."

"That'd certainly make it harder for him to be mad at us," Frank agreed.

Ann recognized her own words coming back to her and leaned over to give Benny a big hug just as the sales clerk spotted them and sidled over.

"Can I help you kids with something?" he asked.

"We'll take this one," all the kids replied, pointing to the Frigidaire "Flair."

Armed with the color swatches in the oven brochure and paint chips they got from the Sears paint department, they stopped at the fabric store to pick out some drapery fabric that matched well with the blue color on the range and the other colors they had chosen for the walls, ceiling,

209

and trim, and then a quick stop at Woolworth's to buy a bunch of paper coin-rolls.

Once home, everyone worked like an assembly line sorting, counting, and rolling Matty's treasure.

Their dad called in the middle of their coin rolling session—Frank answered.

"Oh, hi Dad! Sure, everything is *great* here—how are you? You're... between meetings? Missus Hatchfield...? Sure—hang on."

Frank took the phone away and mock-yelled, "Missus Hatchfield! Phone for you!"

He waited a few seconds.

"I honestly don't know where she is, Dad—I thought she might be in the laundry room, but I guess not? You know, she doesn't hear so good. Um-hum. Yup, were all fine. Well... you don't want to be late for your meeting. I'll tell her. We will—bye, Dad!"

When they finished coin-rolling, Matty's contribution exceeded all expectations with a whopping grand total of sixty-two dollars and seventy eight cents. Everyone applauded when Matty filled in his contribution on the bar chart.

After that, Frank and Randy wrestled the old range out of its pocket and they cleaned around and behind it. When the new range arrived, the delivery men slid the Flair right in, then carted off the old scorched hulk.

Lynn's cousin, the carpenter, a handsome and charming young man named Peter, arrived shortly after the delivery men left to make a bid on the cabinet work. After seeing the new modern range and their older style cabinets, he suggested, in addition to fixing the burned ones, that he could re-face the rest of the cabinets and drawers with a more contemporary look that would more closely match the modern look of the new range.

"It will make your whole kitchen look custom-built and brand new!" he offered.

"That sounds *really* nice, Peter, but we simply can't afford that," Ann admitted.

Peter had also noticed Ann, and she had already decided she didn't mind at all that he had.

"Maybe we can work something out," Peter offered back.

"Let's talk over a piece of cherry pie and coffee," Ann suggested. Peter knew from talking to Lynn that Ann had won the cooking contest and said he felt honored to share a piece of her award-winning pie.

Ann blushed.

"How'd this fire happen, anyway?" he asked.

Feeling she could trust Peter, Ann spilled the beans on their whole story: their dad being out of town, submarining Mrs. Hatchfield, Benny's injuries, the fire... *all of it.*

"Maybe I can help you," Peter offered. "I need pictures of a high-end kitchen project as an example of my work... and... well, maybe, with some help from you and your brothers, plus, some lunches thrown in and say... a date... maybe?"

Ann blushed again. "Okay. And I'll throw in an apple pie, too."

Ann agreed to have him reface all the kitchen cabinets and drawers—and to go out on a date with him, "If we could get a reasonable discount?"

Peter, eager to impress Ann, offered to do it all for only $50 more than his earlier estimate, and to help them smooth out and patch the bubbled ceiling and to pitch in on painting, "for *two* pies."

211

It was too good to pass up—and Ann was also smitten with Peter.

"Deal," Ann offered her hand to shake.

While Ann was busy negotiating kitchen remodeling and her love life inside, the boys all decided to focus on cleaning up both the front and back yards outside.

Benny, Matty, and Tony weeded everything and cleared away general rubbish while Randy and Frank trimmed hedges and removed anything dead. Once the lawns were weeded, Frank mowed them, Randy trimmed them, and Tony found a bag of granulated fertilizer and a bottle of fish emulsion in the garage. The fish emulsion stunk to high-heaven, so Tony, Benny, and Matty stuck with the granulated stuff to feed the lawns and bedding plants before they hosed off the walks and patios and turned the sprinklers on to give the yard a good drink.

With the more expensive stove and the added cost of new cabinet doors in addition to the original cabinet repairs, Ann had to considerably lengthen their bar chart, which meant her chicken paprikash on rice dinner (cooked to perfection on the new range) was overshadowed by an argument with her brothers once Tony noticed what she had done to the chart and pointed it out to the others.

"You just made *way more work* for everyone else without consulting us *first*," he complained. "It's totally *unfair!*"

"But Peter's giving us a *really great* deal, you guys. He's trying to *help* us," she argued back. "I thought you guys would be pleased! He's even gonna help us paint for *free!*"

"Still, we *all* put all our own savings in the pot, so it shoulda been a *group* decision," Randy reminded.

"Well, to be fair to *myself*," Ann defended, "*I* put in more of my savings than the rest of you."

"No, you didn't," Frank corrected her, "*Matty* did."

He had her there.

"Okay," Ann conceded, "then... Matty—what do *you* think?"

She smiled sweetly at him with pleading eyes while Matty contemplated his moment of power and smiled back.

"I'm with Ann," he decided, "I like the fancier kitchen. But I have something fancier I want to add too."

"Like what?" Benny asked, furrowing his brow.

"I'll make a drawing," he answered cryptically, "Then you can all see."

"But—what will it *cost*?" Frank pressed.

"I dunno."

"It's only fair," Tony shrugged. "Let's wait and see Matty's drawing."

That argument went on hold while Matty went off to draw and the others cleared the table and did the dishes so they could start another family brainstorming session on how to make *even more money*—and *quickly*.

"We need an invention like the light bulb or the paper clip," Randy sighed in frustration. "You know... something that doesn't cost a lot to make but *everyone* wants it. Getting lots of people to only spend a little each can add up to a fortune fast."

"We don't have time to *invent* something," Benny sighed back, rolling his eyes at his brother.

The group had settled into a quiet funk when Matty returned with his drawing. He placed it on the table and his siblings gathered around to scrutinize, preparing to argue.

"*This* is what I want to add to the list of improvements," Matty stated. He gave each of his siblings a determined eye: "It's my price for going along... and sharing my treasure."

They all looked at the drawing, each smiling and nodding.

"You know," Frank concluded, "I really *like* this idea, Matty! Why not?"

"All those in favor?" Matty asked, which was answered by unanimous approval.

"Now that *that's* settled," Ann stated, "how are we gonna earn enough money to pay for it all?"

"Maybe we could set up a theater in the garage and screen your movie," Tony suggested to Randy. "Charge everyone a quarter to get in? That would add up pretty quick."

"That's a good idea," Frank agreed. "Or at least, *half* of a good idea. I could put on a laser light show too and we could charge *double* for both."

"What if," Ann started, then stopped, rising from her chair to pace the floor before continuing. "I think those are both great ideas. What if we all, *each of us*, do *similar* stuff, you know—have some sort of *big event* together. I have tons of eggs and flour and baking stuff I got from that dumb contest. With the two ovens I could bake enough stuff for a *huge* bake sale in no time!"

"A carnival!" Matty whooped. Let's have a big Christmas Carnival with games and tickets and prizes!"

"We'll charge an entrance fee and then charge again for all the different stuff inside too!" Randy mused. "That'll add up."

They sat down to draft a plan of attack and schedule, then spent the rest of the evening painting signs to advertise their Christmas Carnival with movies, games, and tasty treats. They would need a day to set up and a day for the event, which would leave them three more days to then get all the cleaning and home improvements done.

The next day Oak Drive and the surrounding neighborhoods were entertained by a bicycle parade of Benjamins dressed in holiday regalia—each bike had red and green streamers woven into their spokes and held a different colorful sign advertising the various events at their "Colossal Christmas Carnival" to be held in their back yard the following day.

Matty, seated on Ann's book rack, rode at the front with her, while they played Christmas music from Frank's tape machine. Randy and Tony rode side by side in the middle holding a large banner between them. Frank brought up the rear, pulling Benny in the wagon, who hollered through a cardboard megaphone, "Tomorrow! One day only! Come one, come all!"

The rest of the day they spent scrounging through their old toys and comic books for little things they didn't really want anymore, to use for booth prizes. Later, Benny and Matty helped frost, ice, and decorate mountains of baked goods while Ann continued filling the kitchen with cupcakes, cookies, cakes, and pies faster than her brothers could consume them.

Meanwhile Frank, Randy, and Tony set up the various booths and events out in the yard. They recruited a couple of neighborhood friends to help, bribing them with some of Ann's still-warm gingerbread cookies.

Peter stopped by on the pretext of double-checking some measurements and was recruited by Ann to help make and wrap red and green popcorn balls.

Randy and Tony set up the garage with rows of benches and folding chairs for their makeshift theater, blocking out light from the garage door with tarps. Randy hung and theatrically lit his rocket model from the rafters as decoration and Frank arranged and mounted every mirror he could find for his laser show all about the room.

By sunset, the back lawn was set up with a crossbow-plunger shooting gallery, a kissing booth for Tony to man, a dime toss with well-waxed plates, tables under the awning for all Ann's baked goods, a water balloon toss where Benny's head would be the target, and around the far side of the house, Matty's Menagerie of Exotic Animals—which would consist of a radioactive Mommacat, who they had dyed green using food coloring, Chaos, who they had bathed and then trimmed down to have a mane and tail tuft in order to pass off as an albino lion, Goopy the Wonder Slug (Matty's newest adopted pet), and Randy's rats, who were... well... the famous *Killer Rats From Outer Space.*

The kids were exhausted, but pleased with what they'd been able to accomplish in a single day.

"But will anyone come?" Benny asked, saying aloud what everyone else was thinking.

When Frank and Randy went out the next morning at around 8:30 AM to hang the big banner announcing the "Colossal Christmas Carnival--25¢ Entrance Fee" across the garage door they were shocked to see a line already forming at their back gate and by the time 9:00 rolled around and they were ready to open there was a line already halfway down the block of both kids and adults. Even old Mr. and Mrs. Winter were waiting there!

"Holy Cow!" Benny exclaimed as he put on his rain

poncho and hobbled over on his crutches to take his seat behind the water-balloon-toss-board and become a living target. "I'm gonna be drowned!"

"I'll trade you places," Tony offered, not all that keen on having to spend an entire day kissing every weird girl in the neighborhood for money.

Ann sat under a banner proclaiming her an official "Future Homemaker of America" and beneath that, "Baked goods direct from a Champion's kitchen!" She had to keep a careful watch as neighborhood kids tried to filch too many freebees from the bowls of broken cookie samples she had placed at the front of her table, while simultaneously guarding the bucket under the table next to her feet, where the soup cans of coins and bills that were collected at each booth were emptied. She was astounded how quickly the bucket began to fill. For her part, she charged top dollar for her baked goods, and used her trophy to collect her money. The pies and cakes all sold out by noon, the popcorn balls by two, and every last cookie and cupcake by three.

Meanwhile, Peter showed up and installed the new cupboards above the new stove and began the long task of removing and replacing all the old cabinet doors. Ann set up her sewing machine on the kitchen table so the two of them could flirt with each other while they worked.

Outside, each booth kept a constant line of customers and Matty's Menagerie was a surprise hit, especially with adults with small children, who decided it was just too adorable to miss.

Tony was glad he kept a tube of ChapStick handy.

Lots of Benny's classmates who liked to tease him cycled through his booth multiple times for chances to nail him with water balloons. He helped to keep them coming back by making snotty faces and shooting insults at all of

217

them.

His faces and Tony's heartthrob lips were pretty evenly profitable commodities.

Randy's movie though, *Killer Rats From Outer Space*, was the hugest hit of all with young and old alike, and following it with Frank's laser show, *Lasers: Ray Guns of the Future*, the two boys played to standing-room-only crowds all day long.

Mrs. Coe couldn't help being distracted by the steady stream of foot traffic filing past her house toward the Benjamins and the noise of laughter and chatter from their back yard.

"*Now* what are they up to?" she complained.

"Why don't you leave those poor Benjamin kids alone, Joy. They're not hurting anyone," Mr. Coe advised.

"The fact they continually attack your son means *nothing* to you?"

Mr. Coe rolled his eyes and mumbled, "Kids fight. It's what they do," as he went back to his paper.

"Ross, come here," Mrs. Coe commanded. "I want you to go over there and find out what they're up to."

"But I thought you told me never to..."

She flicked her index finger on the side off his skull.

"Oow!" he yelped and rubbed the spot.

"Don't sass me—now **GIT!**" and she shoved him out the door.

Ross paid his twenty five cents to enter, figuring his mother would have to reimburse him since she made him her spy. Another screening of the movie and laser show was about to start just as he arrived, so he paid another fifty cents to see it.

Ross and the rest of the crowd watched as Tony, an astronaut on a spacewalk, encountered alien killer rats that chewed their way into his ship and were brought back to wreak havoc on Earth. Randy intercut Tony spewing fake blood with close-ups of the troll doll's feet being chewed to bits—it was hilariously silly and got huge laughs. Lots of blood throughout. Each of the Benjamin kids wrestled with alien rats, lost their battles, and died humorously horrible deaths, and Ann managed to give him a perfect blood-spewing and blood-curdling scream. His ending, where the humans create an army of radioactive cats to devour the rats and save the Earth was followed by the possibility that even more rats were now growing inside the radioactive cats—ending on a shot showing a very pregnant Mommacat with the supertitle double-exposed over it: THE END???

This was followed by Frank's slick presentation, in which he explained how lasers worked and their many practical uses, first burning a popsicle stick in two and then bouncing light around a series of overhead mirrors to create an elaborate latticework of light to *oohs* and *aahs*.

Ross continued into the yard after that, waiting for his eyes to adjust to the sun and not sure what to do next. He checked his pocket change. He only had a dime left and tried the crossbow shoot. He didn't hit the target. That's when he finally saw Benny—the human target. It was too good to be true.

Benny saw Ross coming.

Ross cut to the front of the line and picked up a balloon.

"Cough up a dime first, Bosco!" Benny taunted.

Ross knocked over the neighbor girl, Karen, who was collecting the dimes for Benny's booth, and hurled the balloon anyway, nailing Benny square in the face.

Ross laughed, "Make me!"

Benny got up from his post and hobbled over on his crutches, ready for another fight... then reconsidered.

"That was a pretty nice shot," Benny complimented instead, "but... you still owe us a dime."

"Tough crap. I don't got a dime!"

Benny thought a moment—then asked, "Well, you wanna *help* instead? You won't have to pay if you take my place for a while. It's fun—you just make faces at all the other kids and try to get them to throw balloons at you."

Ross looked around the yard—everyone was having such a good time. He never got to do fun stuff like this.

"Unless you're *scared*," Benny added.

"Who's *scared*! Yeah, okay. But just for ten minutes—a penny a minute!"

"Deal," Benny agreed, nodding. He helped Karen up and had her hold his crutches while he wriggled out of the rain poncho and handed it to Ross.

"I need to go use the bathroom anyway," Benny remarked, then yelled, "Hey, everyone! Now's your chance to bean Bosco!"

Ross took his place behind the sign and began taunting everyone, as the already long balloon toss line quickly doubled.

"You'll never hit me! You're all gonna miss!" Ross mocked, sticking his tongue out at each of them.

Benny smiled to himself as he hobbled back into the house, through the laundry room, and quietly slipped into the garage behind the movie screen to grab the bottle of fish emulsion fertilizer and a small funnel off the tool bench. He went back to the laundry room sink, put a clothespin on his nose, pulled an unblown balloon out of his pocket, put the funnel into the neck of the balloon, and blurped a couple of big blobs of the putrid gunk into the balloon. He then filled the rest of the balloon with water and tied it securely. He thoroughly rinsed the funnel and the sink before he took off the clothespin, but the residual smell still made him gag.

Benny returned to his balloon-toss booth and, handing Karen one of his own dimes, winked at the next kid in line and asked him if he could take cuts.

"Benjamin-Benjamin! Benjamin-Benjamin! *Mnnwah!*" Ross taunted, sticking out his tongue at him.

Then Benny realized it was Bob Ladolo at front of the line. Bob was a couple of years older than him and the Little League pitcher. Benny reconsidered.

"Never mind, you were next," Benny said.

He stepped back and handed Bob his stink bomb.

"Whatever you do, don't miss," he whispered with a wink. "Trust me, you won't be disappointed. And I'll throw in an extra fifty cents as a prize if you bean him."

Bob grinned and nodded back.

Bob summoned every ounce of strength and coordination he could possibly muster, and sent the stink-bomb sailing.

Ross had his mouth open and his tongue out in a taunt when the balloon hit him square in the face with a spectacular splat, drenching his head and shoulders in brown liquid.

A cheer rose from the ranks.

Then, after a pause, "*Eeeeewwww!!!*"

All the kids pinched their noses, gagged, and backed away as the wretched smell of the dead fish goop permeated the air.

Ross bolted up, knocking the plywood board over, turned a sickly green and started spitting and screaming. He stripped off the stinky poncho and dashed from the yard to a round of applause and jeers, and Benny yelling after him, "You're all paid up, Bosco!"

Benny *clink-clinked* a couple of quarters into Bob's hand, but Bob gave them back.

"You're a sick kid, you know that?" Bob grinned in twisted admiration.

Benny nodded in agreement' "I know."

"Looks like this booth is closed for the day," Benny told the other kids, with a smile—but none of them seemed to mind. The afternoon was winding down anyway, and now with the unfortunate smell, people were ready to call it a day.

Mrs. Coe heard Ross's screams from inside the house and intercepted him on the front porch. Ross kept screaming, crying, gagging, and having trouble getting the words out.

Mrs. Coe held her nose and made a face.

"What is that horrid...!"

"They hit me... with a... ba... a bahhh... a... a... *Blaaaaahgh!*" Ross sputtered as he puked on his mother and their porch.

The smell of vomit and dead fish guts was too much for Mrs. Coe, who spontaneously threw up too, joining him in his misery.

Ann paid off their neighborhood helpers in Christmas cookies and cupcakes she had set aside along with Peter's two pies. Then the Benjamin kids poured their massive bucket and wads of cash onto the living room floor to sort, roll, and count in front of the TV.

Frank gasped when he finished adding up the grand total. Even he couldn't believe it.

"We made over *three hundred dollars*?" he wheezed out. "Seriously—this is *unbelievable!*"

"You know what this means?" Ann said, beaming. "It means we can do *everything*! We can paint, pay off Peter, Matty's idea, even replace the emergency fund, and *still* have money to do whatever *else* we want!"

"You know what... let's totally blow Dad's mind," Frank laughed. "Like... we'll super-clean the house, replant the poinsettias in front, fix all the Christmas lights and have the house all decorated up, then we'll all dress up in our Sunday clothes, the works... make this the best Christmas ever!"

Everyone responded with enthusiastic *Yeah*s except Ann, who was *really* miffed that *her* idea that no one but Benny wanted to do when she brought it up was now *Frank's* **great** idea... and **now** everyone **did** want to do it? Then she had to remind herself to be happy that she was getting what she wanted most for Christmas, so she clammed up and simply rolled her eyes at her brothers instead.

"Let's make this the *best* Christmas *ever*," Benny repeated with a big grin from his crutches, while sitting at the hearth.

Randy looked at him sitting there, laughed, and mocked, in a cockney accent, "And God bless us, everyone, eh, Benny?"

223

Chapter Eleven

The Christmas Miracle

The next day felt like all six of them had just won the lottery.

Ann called a window cleaning service and a carpet cleaning service. Frank organized Matty, Benny, and Tony so the four of them cleared things away to prepare for the carpet cleaners to do their job and then they stripped all the beds to launder all the linens and then remake them.

Randy was on furniture duty, waxing every stick of furniture in the house to a glowing sheen.

Tony cleaned the ashes out of the fireplace and set up fresh logs.

Both the window and carpet cleaning teams showed up by nine to begin working inside and out. Meanwhile Ann, Benny, and Matty dashed back to Sears to buy gallons of different colored paints and painting supplies, replacement bulbs for the strings of Christmas lights, and stopped at the nursery for a half a dozen large poinsettias and a very large potted fern in a colorful glazed pot.

Once home, Peter arrived and finished installing the last of the new cupboard doors and stylish new hardware, then taped plastic tarps over all of them to protect them as they all painted the kitchen ceiling, then the walls and finally the trim with pale blue tones to match the range and a butter-yellow window trim color that matched perfectly with Ann's new drapery and tablecloth fabric.

Ann had the carpet cleaning service also steam-clean all the living room furniture and the armchair in their father's bedroom before they left.

After the paint dried and all the tarps were removed, Frank and Randy stripped the kitchen floor and re-waxed it to a high gloss.

The final result was breathtaking—the kitchen looked like something straight out of a *House & Garden* magazine. Peter wanted pictures of his work and asked Ann to be his model, so she scooted off to doll up a bit so she could pose for him in the different shots.

The window and carpet cleaners weren't thrilled when they were paid with rolls of coins, but what could they do? Cash is cash.

Meanwhile the boys went from room to room sorting and organizing closets and drawers, scrubbing all the bathrooms to a high polish, and generally sprucing everything up to "Greeta clean."

Finally, after Ann deliberately kept Matty occupied in the kitchen for part of the afternoon helping her polish the silver, Tony came in and told Matty he had a visitor at the front door.

Matty went to find out who could be asking for him.

Instead, he found the rest of his siblings gathered in the entryway. Not the plain, old entry way, but the new one Matty had reimagined in his drawing.

They had painted it a pale sage green color, as his drawing had indicated, and had placed the large live potted fern in its colorful ceramic pot at the base of the stairwell, right where he wanted it. Matty's agenda was to make the new entryway and fern the perfect place for his new pet slug, Goopy, to call home.

Now it was real. His drawing was *real*.

"It's perfect," Matty beamed. "I need to get Goopy and show him his new home. Thanks, everyone!"

And he rushed back to the kitchen to retrieve his pet.

Benny trimmed the rest of Chaos's fur to get rid of the lion's mane and tail and Tony and Matty gave him a good bath. Everyone was *shocked* to see that Chaos was actually hiding a quite handsome looking hound under all that stained and matted hair. *Who knew?*

When they all set down to meatloaf dinner, with an extra seat at the table for Peter, who everyone decided earned the right to be an honorary Benjamin for the day, every inch of the house was immaculately clean and tidy.

"Tomorrow is Christmas Eve," Ann sighed, proudly. "And we *made it*, we did it—we got *everything* done! Dad's plane lands at five, so he won't be home until around six. That means we have the whole day tomorrow to decorate, and for me to cook the best Christmas Eve dinner *ever*."

"Uh-oh," Benny interjected. "We... forgot something."

"What?" Ann asked, puzzled.

Frank scanned the list and shook his head.

"Nope. We got everything."

"A tree—we didn't get a *Christmas tree*."

All of the kids slumped, suddenly realizing they had completely forgotten about the tree.

"We still have time to get one tomorrow. How much money do we have left?" Randy asked Frank.

Frank went to the desk and looked in the cigar box.

"Only the emergency fund... some loose change, and a couple more penny rolls?" he sighed, counting, then shook his head. "A dollar sixty-three. Not enough for a tree."

"Dad would *not* consider a Christmas tree an emergency," Tony concluded.

Ann thought for a moment, then lit up.

"Wait! It's *perfect*!" she beamed. "We'll have all the ornaments out and the tree stand waiting when Dad gets home. When he sees all the amazing stuff we've done to the house, with a big dinner all set up and ready to eat, I'm sure he'll be up for all of us going out after dinner to buy a tree and decorate it together, as a *family!*"

I don't know..." Frank pondered, skeptical.

"Trust me," Ann replied, then added, "*Trust Dad.*"

The next day was like one of Ann's daydreams made real.

They played Christmas albums on the stereo all day while Frank and Randy planted the poinsettias out front, gave the now-greener lawns one final mowing, hosed the walks and patios clean, and replaced all the dead bulbs in the light strings with fresh ones. Ann spent most of the day in and out of the kitchen, cooking and setting her Christmas Eve table, with Benny and Matty assisting.

Tony draped garlands down the stairway railing and set up the crèche on the mantle, hung the stockings, and stacked the boxes of Christmas ornaments and their tree stand neatly in the corner of the living room to await the tree.

All of them folded and scissored snowflakes and covered every inch of one living room wall with them. They strung popcorn garlands, made more construction-paper ornaments, wrapped presents, took turns bathing and gussying-up in their Christmas finery, with the boys in pressed shirts, coats, and ties and Ann in a tulle-fluffed Dior-style dress with dyed-to-match shoes, ate gingerbread and drank hot cider, and mostly shared the spirit of Christmas together.

As the sun began to set and the ham topped with pineapple rings and cherries, baked sweet potatoes, and fresh-baked dinner rolls, began to fill the house with wonderful, sweet and savory aromas, they all felt nervously excited. They had worked together, and working together had *worked*. Their mother was right: their combined curiosity, creativity, and craft truly had it *all* covered.

What could go possibly wrong?

Mrs. Coe opened her door to a very stern looking man and woman.

"Hello," she said, greeting them.

"Hello, Missus Coe?' The stern woman replied. "We're from juvenile services."

"Yes, I've been expecting you—please come in."

As Nat King Cole finished, "Chestnuts Roasting on an Open Fire," Benny stood vigil at the front window.

"He's home!" Benny announced.

Tony lit the fire.

Randy started a fresh record album.

All of them gathered at the window to see their dad pay the taxi, collect his suitcases, and stride up the front walk.

"Told you we'd pull it off without a hitch," Frank beamed.

"Who's *that*?" Matty asked, as another somewhat familiar car pulled up to park where the taxi just departed.

"Missus Hatchfield's car...?!" Ann gasped.

"And who's... *that*?!" Tony asked as another car

229

pulled up to park in front of hers.

Dr. Vance stepped out of that car.

"And *that*...?!" Benny pointed, as Mrs. Coe approached leading the stern couple their way, with Ross tagging along behind.

"We're all gonna die," Randy gulped.

Ed entered the house, "I'm ho..."

Randy nearly knocked him over, diving past his father to quickly close the door—and *lock* it—*and* put the chain on it as Ann took his arm and drew him away from it.

"Hi Daddy!" Ann chirped. "Welcome home!"

Matty sidled up to his father and tugged on his coat, drawing his attention too.

"Dad, can I have a penny?"

"That depends... were you a good boy while I was gone?" Ed laughed, hoisting Matty in his arms.

"Maybe...?"

He set Matty down, took in the living room, and whistled.

"Well, the house looks *great*. I saw that you guys even fixed the Christmas lights and planted poinsettias," he grinned, but his grin waned as he sensed something was... odd.

He finally registered the now-green, freshly painted front entry adorned with a fern, and his mouth gaped.

"Merry Christmas, Dad...?" Randy offered as a lame explanation, then added out of self-preservation, "It was *Matty's* idea."

"Where's... Missus Hatchfield?" Ed asked.

230

There was a knock on the door, followed by the doorbell. That was followed by some insistent pounding.

Ann gripped her father's arm, pulling him toward the kitchen with, "We'll get that. You must be exhausted and *hungry*—Christmas Eve dinner's all ready and waiting...."

"Isn't that Mrs. Coe's voice on the porch?" Ed questioned.

He pulled his arm free and crossed to the door, pushed Randy aside, pulled off the chain, and opened it wide.

Mrs. Hatchfield, Dr. Vance, *and* Mrs. Coe accompanied by the stern couple and Ross all stood waiting there.

"...completely *unruly* and *unsupervised*!" Mrs. Coe finished addressing the stern couple.

Ed took in the small crowd, baffled.

"And they tried to *poison* me!" Ross added.

"Shut up, Ross!" Mrs. Coe snapped, continuing as she pushed past Ed and into the house. "And as you can see this house is absolutely..."

"Spotless," the stern woman observed sticking her head in through the open door, then making a note of it on a clip board she carried.

"As are the children," the stern man added.

The stern woman made note of that as well as Mrs. Hatchfield sidled past them all and into the living room, glancing daggers at all the kids.

"I'm glad you are back, Mister Benjamin," Mrs. Hatchfield croaked. "We need to talk."

"What is this all about?" Ed asked her, then offered to the others, "I'm sorry... *please*, come in—all of you. Please."

They entered a warm, cozy, and now showpiece-worthy living room, with a fire crackling in the fireplace,

231

freshly scrubbed and polished furniture and carpeting, and freshly scrubbed and totted-up children, who took seats about the room while grinning nervously.

On the stereo Bing Crosby sang, "There's No Place Like Home for the Holidays."

The stern couple circled the room. The woman made more notes. They stopped to take in the wall of snowflakes.

"Pretty," she decided.

"We all made it together," Matty explained.

"Dr. Vance...?" Ed asked, "What are *you* doing here?"

"Hi, and Merry Christmas," he chuckled warmly, shaking Ed's hand. "I was in the area so I just thought I'd pop by to check on Benny?"

"*Benny...?*"

Ed glanced over, now catching Benny's crutches and cast. His eyes darted nervously from each of his kids to the stern couple, to the Coes, to Mrs. Hatchfield, then back to Dr. Vance.

"Just following up on the hit and run accident?" Dr. Vance continued, glancing at Mrs. Hatchfield and then at the older kids.

The stern couple explored on, wandering toward the kitchen with Mrs. Coe and Ross following.

Ed held up a finger to pause his conversation with Dr. Vance while he nervously trailed after them, with Mrs. Hatchfield and Dr. Vance following him, and finally the kids following them all from a safe distance.

They entered the stunning new kitchen and Ed's jaw dropped. He was struck dumb.

All were bathed in the mouth-watering aroma of Ann's baked ham, sweet potatoes, and dinner rolls being kept warm in the glowing new Flair ovens. Ann slipped past all of them to light the candles on their beautifully set holiday table, completing the Normal Rockwell-worthy tableau.

232

A clean, trimmed, and now rather noble-looking Chaos wagged his tail at them all from the sparkling-clean patio window.

There was not a kitten to be found.

The stern woman, looking less stern by the moment, made more notes.

"You know, boys and broken bones. 'Snips and snails, and puppy dog tails,'" Dr. Vance quipped as he knelt down next to Benny and looked him over. "I don't suppose the police ever caught the guy who hit him?"

Ed felt one of his eyes starting to twitch. He glanced at the stern woman, who had her pen poised to write down whatever he said next.

"You *were* told about the accident," Dr. Vance inquired.

"Aah... of *course*... I knew," Ed replied, adding an awkward chuckle to the end of his lie. "Missus Hatchfield... and the kids told me all about it—*didn't* you, Missus Hatchfield...?"

All eyes turned to Mrs. Hatchfield, who wore a sour, inscrutable look and—the kids had noticed right off—a *wig*.

"He's *lying*," Mrs. Coe interrupted, pointing an accusatory finger at Ed, then at Mrs. Hatchfield. "She wouldn't know what these unruly brats have been up to! Half the time her car is gone and the other half she's holed up in the bathroom!"

Mrs. Hatchfield, who had been shooting odious looks at each of the Benjamin kids, reserved her most odious one for Mrs. Coe.

"Who *is* this **annoying** woman? She's obviously de-ranged," Mrs. Hatchfield countered. She glanced at Ed, at the stern couple, and then glared at the kids.

"One only has to look around to see the *truth* here," Mrs. Hatchfield continued, shooting a narrow-eyed glare at

Frank and Ann, "and... to *respond* accordingly. Now Mister Benjamin, if you'll just *pay me my full wages* I'll be on my way."

"But," Matty blurted.

Tony clapped his hands tightly over Matty's mouth.

"Of course," Ed mumbled back, pulling out his checkbook.

"Benny looks just *fine*, Ed," Dr. Vance said, standing. "Well... I'll be on my way. Merry Christmas, kids!"

"Merry Christmas, Doctor Vance," they chirped back.

"And thank you," Ann added.

The stern woman opened the right oven to admire Ann's ham. The stern man took a deep inhale and smiled.

"Just lovely," the now not-at-all-stern woman noted, taking one last look around the kitchen, including a feel of Ann's attractive, crisp new drapes. "I think we've seen enough here."

Ed handed Mrs. Hatchfield a check.

"Thank you, Mister Benjamin," she replied, before shooting all the kids another icy scowl and scurrying out.

"Uh-huh," Ed responded, in a daze.

Mrs. Coe trailed the stern couple to the door.

"But *surely* you don't believe this house and these people. It's some sort of trick! They're all **lying!**"

"And *he* tried to bash my head in with a *rock*!" Ross hollered, pointing at Benny.

The stern couple glanced over at Benny: hair combed, rosy-cheeked, in his adorable Christmas bow tie and suspenders, propped up on his sad little crutches.

"I know what I *saw*!" Mrs. Coe continued. "This house was a mess! There were cats... and *rats* running wild in here! Garbage everywhere! These children were living like *animals*... and... and..."

"And they tried to **murder me with a toilet plunger!**" Ross screamed.

"**Quiet, Ross!**" Mrs. Coe scolded back, swatting him across the face with a sharp crack to shut him up.

The room went as silent as a tomb while the stern man and woman turned to look at Mrs. Coe, and then Ross.

"Perhaps we *should* speak further," the stern man said to Mrs. Coe, "at *your* house."

A suddenly chastened Mrs. Coe followed the stern couple out the door, mewling, "I don't know what came over me. I've never struck my sweet son like that before. You believe me, don't you? It's this Benjamin house. It's evil! That's what it is... *evil.*"

Once they were gone all Ed had to do was point and his kids quickly sat in a row on the couch. He stared at them as he stood breathing in... then out... then in... for several times before....

"There will be no more *lies* in this house tonight—I want the **absolute** truth," Ed commanded. He turned to Benny first. "Benny, you went off on your own somewhere while I was gone and... got hit by a car?"

"Yessir."

"You're grounded for a month. And Frank and Ann too, for not watching after you.

"Matty—tell me the *truth* now. Was Mrs. Hatchfield here the whole time I was gone?"

Matty stared at the floor and answered, "No-o-o. We made her get the scoots and balded her..."

"Never mind that," Ed interrupted. "You're grounded

for a month for your part in it, and Frank and Ann another month for instigating it." He turned to Tony. "And you, young man, can tell me what happened to the *kitchen*...?"

"It caught on fire?" he sighed, adding, "But we *fixed* it."

"You're grounded for a month, and Frank and Ann another month for not preventing it." He turned to Randy. "Randy!"

"Present."

"How much money is left?"

"A dollar sixty-three," Frank answered.

"I asked Randy!" Ed growled.

"A dollar-sixty-three," Randy repeated. "But we still have the emer..."

Ed interrupted him with an upheld hand, "You're grounded for a month—and Frank and Ann *another* month for being so irresponsible."

Ed paused for a beat. He scanned the kids left and right, then took a breath.

"You kids *really* messed up this time. You nearly destroyed the house and could have all ended up in *foster care*! You could have lost me my job! Made the house *unsellable*! And one of you could have been **killed!**" he added, pointing to Benny.

Ed turned away and walked toward the fireplace. He saw the crèche, momentarily distracted by the memory of the day when he and Ellen purchased it during their very first Christmas together, recalling all the hopes and dreams they had shared for their lives back then.

Then his eye caught the row of six empty stockings in need of filling, making him rue this moment and that she left him with this damned flock of kids.

He set his jaw and continued.

236

"I'm *ashamed* of every last one of you—and your *mother* would be ashamed of you too. There won't be any Christmas Eve supper for you tonight. Go straight to your rooms. I'm... *sick of the sight of you.*"

The kids slowly and mournfully rose from the couch, all except Ann. She rose too, but stood, fists clenched, glaring at her father.

He glanced back at her, bristling.

"I said go to your room!"

"Not till I'm ready!" Ann sassed back.

"I have nothing more to say to you."

"Well, I have a **whole lot** to say to **you!**"

The rest of the kids hesitated on the stairs. They turned back to listen as Ann stomped to the middle of the room to face her father.

"So... we're bad kids and you're ashamed of us?! Ashamed of **what?!** That we took care of ourselves? That we've been basically taking care of ourselves since Momma died? That we've all had to handle big problems that normal kids shouldn't have to handle?

"It doesn't matter to you that Missus Hatchfield was a mean, chain-smoking, lazy old cow, or that she *murdered* Lugee! Or that she *just now* stole your money! It doesn't matter to you that Benny went off to the store on his own because he wanted to buy *you* a present! Or that I'm the only girl in my high school that has to raise a family and keep my grades up high enough to get into college and out of this *trap* I'm in," Ann ranted, beginning to tear up.

"You don't care that we all spent all our *own money* and our *entire* Christmas vacation raising enough *more* money to fix the *damned* kitchen and pay for a new stove— that we fixed **everything!**"

Ann took a step closer to her dad and looked directly at him through her tears.

"You say Momma would be ashamed of us... but you're **wrong**. Momma would be **proud** of us. Proud that we all stuck together and took care of each other and love each other. The one she'd be ashamed of... is **you**."

Ann backed up, sobbing.

"You're the one who stopped caring. Who's never around anymore, who wants to sell our home, our family home, that we fought for and worked for and grew up in and *she* was in."

Ann burst into tears and ran up the stairs past her brothers, continuing, "When Momma died... it's like... *you died too!*"

Ed heard Ann's door slam.

His own eyes began to well with tears. He crossed to the entryway closet, grabbed his overcoat, and left, closing the front door behind him.

Ann went down later to put all the food away only to find her brothers had already done it for her.

She looked around their beautiful new kitchen, her lovely unused table setting, the sparkling clean house, and wept again.

She looked out the front window. Her father's car was still gone.

Why can't he see?

She returned to her bedroom and had a more serious, somber cry into her pillow.

She dug out her diary from between her mattresses to write. But she couldn't put any of it into words. For the first time since her mother's death, Ann found herself bitterly angry with her. Angry at her for dying, for leaving them *all*, and *yes*, for telling her to, "Take care of your dad and brothers." Who says that to a *kid*? Who makes a young girl responsible for raising all her siblings and caring for her surviving parent?

It was suddenly clear how grossly unfair an expectation it was for her mother to place on her. She sighed and wrote:

December 24, 1966

Despite it all, everything went wrong. There's still no Christmas this year. No tree. No Santa. Dad is madder at us than ever.

I did my best, we all did our best, probably better than anyone else our ages could have ever done, but even together we still failed.

I'm sorry we all failed you, Momma.

There was a knock on her door. Ann tucked the diary under her pillow.

The door creaked open.

It was Matty.

He crossed to Ann's bedside. She rolled over to face him as he handed her a drawing.

"Why are you still up, honey? You should be in bed."

"But I made this for you."

Ann looked at it.

It was a crayon sketch of their house with all of them standing in front of it, smiling. Chaos, Mommacat, and the rats were there too. And Goopy.

Their Dad was there with all of them, standing right behind them all and smiling proudly. The poinsettias and Christmas lights were all there—it was Matty's fantasy version of a perfectly Merry Christmas.

In the starry sky right above the house, Matty had

cut out an oddly shaped hole in the paper. Ann felt the hole with her finger, and asked, "What's this?'

Matty took the drawing from her and leaned it up against the lamp on her bedside table.

Light spilled through the hole, which revealed itself to be a glowing, winged figure.

"Oh! It's a Christmas angel," Ann sighed.

Matty shook his head.

"It's Momma."

"Thank you, Matty," Ann choked out, overcome with emotion. She gave him a hug.

"You should go back to bed now, sweetie. Santa Claus will be here before you know it."

Matty left.

Ann stared at the marvelous drawing he gave her, with their glowing mother keeping vigil over them, feeling closer to her brothers and her mother than she ever had before and trying to cling to her last ounce of hope until her eyes grew heavy with sleep.

"Get up! Get up! It's **Christmas!**" Matty and Benny screamed, pounding on everyone's bedroom doors at the crack of dawn, with Benny using a crutch to pound extra-loud.

They laughed as Matty felt his way down the still dark stairs carrying a stack of his gifts for everyone, while Benny carefully crutched his way down with a grocery bag full of his gifts.

Matty flipped on the living room lights.

The living room looked the same as when they left it.

Tony came down with his gifts and crossed to the fireplace.

The stockings he had put up hung empty.

Matty scampered to the corner of the room where he stared in disbelief at the boxes of tree ornaments and strings of popcorn still waiting for a tree.

Somehow he had hoped Santa would have made it all right again.

Frank, Randy, and then Ann came down carrying their gifts to give to each other.

The house was dead quiet.

Matty turned to look at Ann, disappointed.

"Santa didn't come," he explained.

All the kids looked upstairs in the direction of their father's room. Not a peep was heard.

"Merry Christmas to all and to all a *good night*," Randy snarked. He dropped his bag of gift for everyone in the middle of the floor and plodded back up the stairs in a pout while Benny stared at the floor, Ann collapsed onto the couch, and Frank rubbed the back of his neck, when they suddenly all heard Matty yell from the kitchen:

"Oh my God! Oh my God! **Oh my God!**"

They all dashed in to find him staring out the sliding glass patio doors.

"Lookie!" he gasped.

The Benjamin kids gathered around the window and gaped.

The entire back yard was full of Christmas trees: tall ones, short ones, fat, full ones, thin, sparsely-branched ones, and even a few flocked ones. It was a Christmas tree forest. The morning sun cut across the forest, giving added dimension, casting long shadows across the lawn.

It had somehow magically appeared there during

the night.

How...?

They slid open the door to explore this Christmas miracle and found hidden in amongst the trees were all their Christmas gifts from Santa.

Ann couldn't believe it. She sat on a patio chair, dumbfounded, tears of joy welling in her eyes.

"They were free," she heard her dad's voice say.

She turned to see a very tired Ed slumped in the far corner of the patio.

"I was driving around and passed a lot that was closing. The guy selling them had 'em all loaded on his truck to take the ones no one wanted to the dump, so I had him bring them here instead," he explained. "Because... well, I *remembered...*"

Ann pulled her chair over next to his and sat.

He put his head in his hands, weeping, and continued.

"I miss your mother so much, Annie... and it just... *hurts* too much. But it finally dawned on me, when I was thinking about all you kids—how *like her* you all are. She was clever like Frank, and funny like Randy, Tony has her sweet smile, Benny has her moral spirit, Matty, her creativity..."

He turned to Ann, "And you, well... the nicest thing anyone could ever say about you is you're *just like your mother.*"

"Oh, Daddy," Ann wept, leaning over to hug him.

"She's still here with us, Annie," he whispered as they embraced. "She's still here with me. She's in all of you kids."

Ed finally let go and pointed to a large, kite-shaped package leaning against the wall next to him.

"That one's for you."

Ann tore it open to find the "For Sale" sign, which

was no longer in the front lawn.

"Oh, Daddy!" Ann sobbed.

From somewhere in the forest, Benny shouted out, "Hey! That one's *mine*," and shoved Matty into one of the tallest trees, knocking it and three smaller ones down like dominoes.

"Nuht-uh!" Matty countered. "There's no *tag*—finders keepers!

Give it *back*!" Benny insisted.

"It could be for me, you know!" Tony posed, entering the fray, and shoving Benny out of the way and into Randy.

"Look who you're shovin', Junior!" Randy groused at Benny, as another tree toppled with a thud.

"Fight-fight-fight...!" Frank taunted.

"You kids behave yourselves in there or there'll be hell to pay!" Ed hollered.

Out in front of the Benjamin house, Mr. and Mrs. Winter were having a Christmas morning stroll when they heard the ruckus and tussling and yelling and scolding coming from the Benjamins' back yard.

"The Benjamins are at it again," Mrs. Winter laughed, winking at her husband.

"The neighborhood just wouldn't be the same without them, that's a fact," Mr. Winter concluded, chuckling back.

Acknowledgements

I am eternally thankful for the help, inspiration, and brainpower of my husband, **Chuck Richardson**, in both the writing and technical crafting of all my books. I also thank **Steve Hulett** and **Asa DeMatteo** for their editorial expertise and sharp eyeballs—they have each and both helped make me a better writer.

Other Books By
Aurelio O'Brien

EVE

EVE transports us to a future as silly as it is stunning, as beautiful as it is earthy; one where all technology has been replaced by biologically designed Creature Comforts™.

The last functioning robot, Pentser, is offended by this turn of events and plots revenge. Pentser induces its lonely human owner, Govil, a genetic designer for this world's sole facilitator, GenieCorp™, into secretly creating a companion for the bio-engineer: a normal, deliberately average woman, Eve. In doing so, Govil violates every law of this new age.

Will Eve learn of her strange origins? Will GenieCorp™ track down the illicit pair, will Pentser's own mysterious plans play out, or will love indeed conquer all?

GENeration eXtraTERrestrial

Dr. Grace Brown, a government research scientist at ELF (the Extraterrestrial Life Forms lab), must investigate a spate of alleged human abductees who believe they have been impregnated by aliens. To punish her boss for this unwanted assignment, Grace brings these nutty abductees back to the lab for "further study," but the joke is on her when each gives birth to different and undeniably non-human offspring. This new generation extraterrestrial is as eccentric as their diverse Earth parents. They cause pandemonium in the government, the courts, and the churches, as the world tries to cope with this unexpected new reality. Grace bonds with and adopts a tiny and brilliant alien boy, Charlie, whose mother died in childbirth. The others return with their Earthly parents to their homes, where they try to grow up as normally as an alien can.

Nature and nurture collide as these children and their families face issues of gender, race, religion, vegetarianism, politics, equality, adoption, alcoholism, love, divorce, sexuality, drug addiction, and fame. These ultimate outsiders must cope with parental love, sibling rivalries, peer pressure, and try to fit in, stand out, and make their way in the world, a world that is not really theirs. All the while one question is never far from their thoughts: will their absent and negligent space-parents return for them someday? Charlie makes it his personal mission to find out.

I WAS A TEENAGE CHEERLEADER

High school senior Rhonda Glock's life is about to change. After being assaulted and bitten by a disgruntled, soon-to-be-ex-cheerleader, the heretofore invisible high school "brainy girl" periodically and eerily transmutes into Ronnie, the most popular cheerleader at Lawrence Talbot High.

No longer awkward and ignored as Ronnie, Rhonda grapples with both fearing and embracing her new, unwanted persona. She experiences a new status high and her first academic failures. She confronts family dramas—the shenanigans of her two mischievous younger brothers—while meeting the expectations of her super-achiever mother. She endures interactions with a spooky lady janitor and her creepy pet Chihuahua (who thinks it is a cat), and the high school milieu, all the while navigating her unrequited love for Bud, her childhood best-friend and the school's favorite football hero.

Hocus-pocus and hijinks abound as Rhonda discovers what it is like to be her own nemesis and romantic rival. Can Rhonda and Bud both learn the truth about the mysteries of real life and true love before the end of the prom?

One thing is certain: by the end of this book—you will believe in magic!

About the Author

Aurelio O'Brien started life in a two-parent, then—*very* sadly—a single-parent family of six kids. He and his original five siblings were raised in the idyllic 1960's suburbia of San Jose, California. A family of odd, creative, assertive, clever, and mostly unsupervised kids, there was no end of fun and madness, and so, no shortage of material to draw upon when writing **Family Trees**. The fun and madness expanded further with the addition of another sister and brother when his family later became a blended step-parent family.

Aurelio's odd mix of talents and childhood experiences led him to a successful career as an illustrator, animator, and graphic designer. With his debut sci-fi novel, **EVE**, he poured his unique observations on life into an enchanting, wry, and deftly penned satire of the future. His second sci-fi novel, **GENeration eXtraTERrestrial**, explored what growing up can be like when you enter the world as a true outsider, with physical characteristics, talents, and thoughts that are more than just a little different from those of your peers. And with **I Was A Teenage Cheerleader**, Aurelio used fantasy to examine teenaged discovery of self and the universal struggles we all have while coming of age in niches that work hard to define us before we have the full capacity to decide for ourselves who we really are and build niches all our own.

     This fourth novel, **Family Trees**, is constructed from Aurelio's nostalgic remembrances of life in the mid-1960's and what truly defined his peculiar family. What they learned from each other and their parents became, for him, the true definition of family. Loosely based on the single-parent period of his life, names were changed to protect the guilty, and although many of the incidences and events are heavily based in reality—he chose to create legend rather than print the facts.

Made in the USA
Middletown, DE
02 December 2020

26019486R00146